Lord, please let this time be different . . .

She'd seen so many men and boys die from such wounds, and she'd been helpless to save them. This time . . . She looked down at the injured man. Dark lashes lay like smudges of soot across his pale cheeks, and the lines around his eyes suggested deep creases when he smiled.

"What's your name son?" the old doctor asked.

"Jordan Cooke," came the terse reply through clenched teeth.

"Looks like someone set out to quarter you and nearly succeeded," Doc continued as he held the needle up to the light, squinted the eye into focus, and shoved the suturing material through.

Though it had been thirteen years since Gabrielle had assisted in an operation, she recognized the techniques of an army surgeon—and a good one.

It seemed hours before Gabrielle was able to move from her cramped kneeling position. As she stood shakily to her feet, Doc flipped up her skirts, pushed up her pantaloons, and proceeded to massage her legs.

"Gotta rub some blood back into your limbs," he explained as she turned from rose to scarlet.

Mr. Cooke had not failed to observe the scene, and while the other men in the pullman car coughed, cleared their throats, or cast their eyes discreetly elsewhere, he continued to stare.

"You're certainly no gentleman," she retorted, "even if you are in a weakened condition."

"You're absolutely right. Being a gentleman got me nowhere, so I gave it up." The effect of a wide smile, imparting an elfin quality to his chiseled features, was wasted on Gabrielle.

She stiffened her back and pivoted her head forward. His voice, though weak, held an accent she had previously missed. She'd slaved, suffered, prayed for, and endured humiliation today to save a murdering, marauding *Yankee*!

WAIT FOR THE SUN

Maryn Langer

BOOKS

of the Zondervan Publishing House
Grand Rapids, Michigan

WAIT FOR THE SUN
Copyright 1985 by The Zondervan Corporation
1415 Lake Drive, S.E.
Grand Rapids, Michigan 49506

ISBN 0-310-46792-6

Edited by Anne Severance

Designed by Kim Koning

Printed in the United States of America

85   86   87   88   89   90   /   10   9   8   7   6   5   4   3   2   1

To my mother and Ken

She gathered close her too-thin cape, grown old,
And hoped for warmth, as she was cold inside.
She reined her gloomy thoughts—too uncontrolled,
While holding to the piece that wasn't tied.
Unwarmed, she muttered, "I'm not satisfied
With this wrap. I must get a better one,
But I will use it waiting for the sun."

She pulled the scanty cape about her more
So that its covering would surely press
New warmth into her chilling skin, before
The sun could move from clouded shadiness
With heat to comfort her, to warm and bless.
The heart within her breast would be warmed too,
She thought, by sunshine that was overdue.

Pearle M. Olsen
from "Frame the Lace Moments"

CHAPTER 1

GABRIELLE SEVIER STOOD untouched by the sea of humanity swirling around and overflowing the platform of the Union Pacific train station in Omaha, Nebraska. Stood in the half-light of predawn that mid-May morning and fretted.

Had she done the right thing, leaving her unmarried sister to support and care for their invalid father while she went West? Went incredibly far West to the Idaho Territory to look after her two little nieces left motherless by the death of her younger sister Ellen?

She had spent many anxious hours on her knees in prayer for help in making the decision, but she never could be sure she heard His answer. His voice was garbled by the tremendous yearnings that filled her heart—yearnings she seemed powerless to remove. The yearning to be free from the grinding servitude and poverty of nursing. The yearning for a life of her own as a proper wife to a husband and mother of his children. Well, her brother-in-law had guaranteed her children and hinted at more.

If the decision was unwise, it was too late for change. She held a one-way first-class ticket to Utah provided by Edward Bailey, and not enough money of her own to purchase a return ticket to Nashville.

This line of thinking was self-destructive and *that* Gabrielle was *not*. Having traveled from Chicago with the newly arrived immigrants, she directed her thoughts and attention to the swarthy men splashing about in buckets under the pump, attempting to wash the stain of travel from their strong, energetic bodies. Confident, assured, never-say-die looks fixed their faces as they shouted their joy in the languages of their varied homelands—German, Gaelic, French, Spanish.

And then she turned toward their women. Such nondescript, pathetic creatures, handkerchiefs hiding their hair, the fabric of their dresses, coarse and faded. Around them, chubby children played hide-and-seek among the boxes, baskets, blue-checked feather beds tied in bundles, and red chests corded with rope.

A lone woman on her knees before a scarred chest, which had burst open on the journey, drew Gabrielle's attention. Its entire contents were spilled onto the station platform. *Everything there isn't worth five dollars*, Gabrielle thought as she surveyed the old, so-coarse clothes, and battered utensils. Yet obviously all was precious to the sobbing woman.

Gabrielle looked down at her own carefully mended cape and, with a properly gloved hand, pulled it closer against the special chill of sunrise. In her palm, she still clutched the two brass claim plates stamped *Kelton, Utah Territory*, afraid that if she let them drop into her small purse, they might vanish and with them all trace of her worldly possessions. *Lord, please watch over what little I have.* With a resigned sigh, she dropped the checks into a corner of the handbag and lectured herself about doing her part by keeping it with her at all times.

The plight of the distraught immigrant woman nagged at Gabrielle. With no idea of what she could do, she started toward her, then noticed two men approaching with hammers and rope. Her conscience relieved, Gabrielle became absorbed in the little scene as though viewing a play.

An unexpected blast from a nearby freight engine knifed through the air. Trembling with the shock, Gabrielle strained to see the reason for this strident intrusion. She focused on a towering man who was directing the loading of a freight car. The impatient warning also startled the men working a winch that suspended a large steel beam. The winch slipped, allowing the piece of metal its momentary freedom, and it swung out, striking the man and sending him sprawling into the dust.

The scene froze. No one moved. The man lay motionless, a dark stain spreading slowly along the shoulder of his jacket. Still, everyone stood hypnotized. Gabrielle cast her eyes about, looking for someone willing to help him. The stricken faces told her no one could. Experience told her he might even now be bleeding to death. Most surely he was rapidly losing consciousness.

The present scene shocked Gabrielle back to a memory of her Tennessee plantation home. She was a girl of fifteen again. Young stretcher-bearers were bringing in wounded soldiers and laying them at her feet. She looked into pleading eyes begging her to heal, to make them whole.

The wounded man groaned. Gabrielle, disregarding her vow to leave nursing forever behind, grabbed the arm of a man holding a washbasin, and pointing at the pump, made clear her need for water. He filled the basin and forced a path for her through the human statues to the injured man's side. She peeled off her gloves and dropped them and her purse into the dust as she knelt, oblivious to the damage to her lovingly

9

restyled traveling suit. She drew back her skirt, intending to tear bandages from her white lace-edged petticoats. Magically, clean white towels appeared and the underskirts were spared.

Her actions broke the spell. Now, clumsy but eager hands were at her bidding. They straightened his body, placed a pillow under his head, spread a blanket over him, and lifted him so the sleeve could be cut off and the coat removed.

Gabrielle pulled his blood-soaked shirt away from the wound and thrust a cold wet towel against the ugly gash. He came to with a groan when she touched him. Jaw clamped, he bore her ministrations in silence. With her free hand she felt the hard ridge of his collarbone, found the pulsing vessel in his neck, and pressed it closed with her thumb. She didn't know how long she stayed crouched over him, blood flowing through the towel, staining her fingers crimson while the other hand continued the intense pressure to stop the flow.

His face faded into that of a boy soldier whose lifeblood had oozed away through her fingers. She had been unable to stanch the flow then, and he had died, there in her house in the last battle of a lost war.

She would not lose this life if she could help it. *Lord, You always hear my prayers for my patients and I recognize Your hand. Please guide me in saving this man's life, if it's Your will.* Feeling renewed, she again focused her attention on the wound. At last, the bleeding seemed to stop. Cautiously she moved her hands away. Watching intently, she sighed in relief. There was no new stream of scarlet.

His eyes came open slowly. They were green, a deep sea-green. But the light was gone from them, and the pupils were enormous. And not even the sun-made copper tan of his skin could hide the pallor underneath. Blue-tinged shadows gathered around his mouth and sweat beaded on his skin. The first rays of morning sun struck hot, but his face was cold and clammy to her touch and his breathing shallow. She could barely find the faint surge of his pulse. He moved, restlessly, and he seemed to be trying to make out the figure who hovered over him.

To spare him the effort, she spoke to him gently, firmly, as one would to a small child. "You mustn't move. You must stay very still. Do you hear me?" Her words sounded clear and strong in the silence which still surrounded the entire area. Even the children made no noise, clutching their mothers' skirts.

The green gaze sharpened for an instant before his eyes closed again. He lay still, save for small involuntary shivers which shook his body. Shock! She needed more blankets. They materialized and gentle hands wrapped them around him. "Water," she said, and a bucket and cup were set beside her. She dripped the water on his lips, and smiled with satisfaction as his mouth opened and he swallowed eagerly.

The man's color was better, his pulse stronger. His breathing grew deep and regular, and his body was no longer gripped by the chilling spasms. She sat back on her heels, aware of rivulets of perspiration running down between her breasts, her shoulder blades, and over her forehead. She reached for a towel and stopped, her hand poised in midair. The hand was caked with blood, slick and red, and she had a hard time claiming it. Someone knelt and washed it in the basin of cold water, bathed her face and dried it.

She watched him fade in and out of consciousness. "Here," she ordered once when he was awake, "drink more water." He turned his head away. "Drink!" Reluctantly this time, he did as she asked. "Have you had anything to eat?"

"No time." His voice sounded pathetically weak.

"You'll feel better when you get some food, but now we need to find a wagon and a doctor. That shoulder needs stitches."

She looked up, expecting to see a wagon standing at the ready. Everything else she needed this morning had appeared instantly, but what she saw was a grizzled old man arriving in a one-seated buggy. He had obviously dressed in great haste, for the buttons on his shirt failed to come out even and a shirttail flapped from under his jacket. He grabbed a small black bag and launched himself from the buggy toward Gabrielle and her patient.

He remained standing, merely bending over for a quick examination. "Can't stitch him up here. Have to get him down to my office."

"Have to be on that train!" It was the forced whisper of the injured man. He clutched his shirt front. "Coat. My coat. Ticket!"

Gabrielle retrieved the remnants of an expensive tweed jacket. The inside pocket contained his ticket. She placed it in his hand and watched the fingers curl protectively around it.

The doctor stood towering over the prostrate form. "You move any distance with that wound and you'll bleed to death, son. It'll never heal without stitches. A good chance you'll get blood poisoning, too. But I ain't gonna treat you here on the ground."

"What do I owe you?" Again the injured man risked Gabrielle's displeasure and reached awkwardly for his money belt.

Gabrielle grabbed his hand and pinned it across his stomach. "Don't you dare move that arm and start it bleeding again."

"Don't owe me nothin'. Wouldn't feel right chargin' a man so all-fired determined to kill hisself." The doctor wheeled about and stalked back to his buggy.

Gabrielle watched him drop his bag on the floor and grab the buggy top support posts as leverage to heave his portly body into the seat. Her heart sank. Her fight today had been as useless as it had been in '65, with one horrible difference. The man lying before her had a choice.

His pupils were still enlarged. He was still in shock, which was, she supposed, the reason for his irrational behavior. Whatever the cause, she had no intention of giving up now. There had to be a solution to this impasse and she intended to find it.

Before she rose from her kneeling position, she petitioned the Lord once more to help her. *He obviously has no sense, Lord, so it's up to us to save him. Help me to know what to do.* She rose to her feet and ran to the buggy. "Isn't there someplace here we could move him?" she heard herself beg. "Maybe into the dining car. The tables would serve as a makeshift operating arena."

"Lady, a man that bent on seein' what's on the other side don't deserve to live. If he don't die today, he'll make sure he finds a way tomorrow." He took out a stained handkerchief and slowly and thoroughly mopped the rivers of sweat pouring from under his hat and disappearing into his shirt collar.

Gabrielle, staring into space and wishing she could thrash some sense into these two stubborn men, let her eyes rest on the rich brown exterior of the Pullman Palace railroad cars. They stood out in such contrast to the drab coaches being boarded by the second- and third-class passengers. "Of course," she said aloud. "Don't you go anywhere!" she ordered the doctor. Walking swiftly back to her patient who was attempting to sit up, she stood over him. "And don't you move a muscle! You start that arm bleeding again and I'll see it's amputated."

She didn't wait to see what effect her bluff had on him, but picked up her skirts and ran to the conductor, resplendent in brass-buttoned blue uniform, standing impressively by the steps of one of the Pullman cars. She explained the stalemate to him. "He has a ticket. Would it be possible to have one of the beds made up? And when the doctor has finished with the stitches, is there a train to bring him back here to Omaha?"

The conductor laughed. "I've had some strange requests but this does beat all. I reckon we can arrange it. There is one problem, though. All the seats are sold, and someone is going to have to stand if that bed is to be left made up."

"Consider my seat the other half of the bed, and I'll make do somehow." She dashed to the waiting doctor and presented her plan, fearing greatly a negative reaction.

To her surprise, he gave her a wide, yellow-toothed grin. "I always wanted to ride in one of them fancy sleeper cars. Heard about 'em from the rich folks I treat in town. Never thought I'd see the inside of one."

"Does that mean you'll do it?"

"Means I'll do it if you can get that stubborn cayuse to agree."

She watched Doc drive his horse and buggy to the shady side of the station and make arrangements for their care before hurrying back to her patient's side.

Kneeling beside him, she told him her plan. "Thanks," was all he said and signaled to an anxious man standing nearby. Gabrielle left them in conversation and moved to recover her personal items. She looked frantically about for her purse. *And I wasn't going to let it out of my sight!* she moaned inwardly. What would she do without her money, ticket, and baggage claims?

"Are you looking for these?" asked a soft voice from behind her.

Gabrielle whirled to face a fashionably dressed, elegantly groomed woman in her middle twenties. She was holding out the gloves and a purse, nearly unrecognizable beneath its layers of dust.

"I'd have cleaned off your purse, but I could see no reason for both of us to ruin our outfits." She smiled, but stood well away from Gabrielle.

Gabrielle looked down at her own suit, so skillfully

and accurately copied from the picture in Godey's Lady's Book by her dressmaker sister, the periwinkle blue of the skirt dulled by dust gathered as she had knelt beside the injured man. Not that she would have done differently, but now she couldn't think how to make herself presentable.

"Your travel valise is there on the platform," the self-appointed guardian angel reminded her. "If you have a whisk broom, perhaps you can persuade someone to brush you off."

Gabrielle claimed her gloves and purse. "Thank you for caring for my belongings."

"That's quite a feat you performed on Jordan. I do appreciate your saving his life. I have a score to even with him on this trip." She tipped her head in a farewell gesture and stepped daintily along the platform to the Pullman car.

Gabrielle watched the conductor greet the young woman as an old friend. *How strange,* Gabrielle thought. *She knows the first name of the injured man and is obviously a frequent passenger on the train. Or maybe she's . . .* But before she could ponder the encounter further, she noticed that the doctor had commandeered a stretcher from somewhere and was now supervising the transporting of his patient aboard the train.

Since Gabrielle's presence was no longer required, she took her benefactor's advice. There, on a small barrel, sat a young girl, hair stringing from under a well-used straw hat, unwashed bare feet dangling above the boards of the floor.

"Would you mind brushing the dust from my skirt?"

The girl surveyed Gabrielle with eyes far older than her years. "It'll cost you a nickel."

Gabrielle was aghast at the impertinence and greed. While a nickel was considerably more than the job was worth, there were no other candidates for the chore. She was sure this little urchin was well aware of the need to board the train very soon, and Gabrielle didn't dare take time to haggle.

Stretching forth a grimy hand, palm up, the child hopped from the keg.

"Not until after you've brushed me off." Gabrielle wasn't going to chance having the little waif grab the money and disappear into the crowd still filling the station platform.

Shaking her head vigorously, the girl planted her feet and continued to stand, hand outstretched.

Gabrielle looked anxiously about. Both patient and doctor were now aboard, and the conductor stood by the steps of his boarding car, looking at the watch in his hand. She quickly retrieved the brush from her valise, jammed her hand into the purse, and choked on the dust clouds that swirled about. Producing the nickel and cramming it into one grubby palm, she thrust the whisk broom into the other. "Now, brush, and be quick about it!"

The child knelt down and attacked Gabrielle's skirt, making the dust fly. Gabrielle held her handkerchief to her face in an attempt to filter air for breathing.

"There," she said at last, and handed back the whisk broom, pausing to issue a warning, "You gonna miss your train, if you don't hurry." She vanished, as Gabrielle knew she would, into the crush of people.

The conductor now faced the front of the train and raised his hand, in a signal to the engineer. Gabrielle felt her heart leap and stick in her throat. She snatched up her valise and made an unladylike dash through the crowd, arriving breathless at the Pullman car into which the doctor and his patient had disappeared. A porter offered her a steadying hand as she clambered aboard. The engine gave its last warning whistle and started a slow smoke-belching pull out of the station.

The porter took her valise and opened the heavy

door into the car. She grasped any available protuberance to steady herself as she made her way down the aisle. When she saw the bed and the doctor bending over the sprawling figure, she remembered she had no place to sit. How lightly she had said she would make arrangements.

"Girl, don't stand there gawkin'!" came the impatient voice of the doctor. "Get yourself washed and bring me a basin of water so's I can get on with this."

The porter showed her the uncurtained washroom. There, Gabrielle took off her hat, cape, and suit jacket, and put on a linen traveling duster as protection from the dust that boiled up from the tracks and in through the open windows. Two men and a boy, sitting in seats across the aisle, stared openly as she washed her face and hands and made minor repairs to her hair. The porter stood in the aisle outside the washroom, holding towels and a deep metal basin filled with warm water. She carried them to the doctor while the porter stored her valise in the compartment behind the seat now made into a bed.

The doctor poured carbolic acid crystals into the water. "Stir until these dissolve. Then, wash around the wound. Won't do no harm if some gets in." And he retreated to the washroom.

She looked down at the injured man. His shirt had been removed and he lay on his back, naked from the waist up. After the War years of working in her home-turned-hospital, the sight of a half-dressed man should not have disturbed her, but it did. She averted her eyes from the lean muscular torso, as tanned as his face. What sort of person was he? She blanked her mind against further speculation, sat on the edge of the berth, and balanced the disinfectant in her lap.

Dark lashes lay like smudges of soot across his pale cheeks, and the lines around his eyes suggested deep creases when he smiled. Or were they acquired by squinting long hours into the sun? Beads of sweat stood out on his upper lip. Although his eyes were closed and his breathing regular, clenched fists told her he wasn't asleep.

"Turn very slowly onto your side facing me," she instructed, "and try to stay as near the edge of the bed as possible."

She wanted to help him turn, but she didn't touch him. Feelings for this nameless man, feelings she could neither explain nor understand flooded through her, and a built-in wisdom acquired through the centuries and retained deep in her inner being warned her. She could only watch as his jaws and mouth clamped tight. Sweat sprang anew on his skin, and his breathing hissed through lips tensed from the effort.

Now she concentrated on bathing the raw wound in preparation for the stitches. It was a deep jagged cut, and the danger of infection was great. She'd seen so many men and boys die from such wounds, and she'd been helpless to save them. *Lord, please let this time be different.*

The doctor returned and bent over to examine the shoulder. "You do good work. Get your nursin' in the War?"

"Yes," she answered briefly, stunned by his kind words. She was usually ignored or verbally abused, never praised.

"Thought so." He eyed the spot where she sat. "Be a good girl and get on the other side of our patient."

The large man filled much of the bed. To do as she had been asked, she would have to crawl over him. Handing the basin to the hovering porter, she bent and slowly removed her shoes. Every eye was trained on the little drama as it unfolded, and nothing would be missed as she made her way across the patient to her assigned spot. She was mentally trying to imagine how she could execute the maneuver without making an unforgettable spectacle of herself. Then, deciding she'd already succeeded in doing just that at the train station, she abandoned further thoughts of etiquette and squirmed across his legs to the other side of the bed as gracefully as petticoats and long skirts would allow.

From this vantage point, Gabrielle could see the sun-streaked blond hair darkened by sweat that rolled down his neck and back. Taking a towel, she dried him, leaving the thick hair mussed and tangled. She couldn't resist smoothing it a bit. It felt like straw, rough and stiff.

"What's your name, son?" the doctor asked.

"Jordan Cooke," came the terse reply through clenched teeth.

"Like to know who I'm sewin' on when possible. See you got a few more scars. You makin' a collection?"

Gabrielle looked closer and could see a long thin line running white against tan, from the top of his shoulder down his back to his waist. *Well, Jordan Cooke. You haven't led a sheltered existence, I see. Looks to me like a bayonet ripped you open. You had a skilled surgeon, or you'd probably be crippled or dead.*

"Looks like someone set out to quarter you and nearly succeeded," Doc continued as he held the needle up to the light, squinted the eye into focus, and shoved the suturing material through. "Can't use chloroform. Put the whole car to sleep in this heat. Have to open the cut up, rub morphine sulphate into it. Then, when the inside's numb, I'll tie off the worst bleeders and sew you back together." Doc spoke as casually as if he were giving instructions on angling for mountain trout. But when he pulled the gash apart, deadened it and began suturing, Gabrielle recognized the techniques of an army surgeon—and a good one. Jordan Cooke was a lucky man.

She was kept busy toweling up blood, but this time

as she held the pressure point, she knew the injury would soon be packed with silver nitrate to speed coagulation before it was securely bandaged. Though it had been thirteen years since she had assisted in an operation, her skills only lay dormant. She wiped the perspiration from the face and eyes of the old doctor and handed him the instruments from their case as he needed them.

She looked once at Jordan Cooke's hand resting on his thigh. The fist was clenched until the knuckles stood out sharp and white. She could only imagine his agony and, helpless to lessen it, wanted to scream a release for him. Losing her concentration, she nearly missed a command from the doctor, and so vowed she would not think about anything but the procedure.

Her body held rigid steadied her against the rocking motion of the train. One hand stopped the blood flow; the other mopped patient and doctor, while her legs, curled under her, began cramping painfully. Gabrielle continued to function only because of the self-discipline which had kept her barren life tolerable. By allowing no thought to surface which did not pertain directly to the matter at hand, she held to her tasks.

"All right, sister, you can let go now."

The words sliced through her concentration, and she released the pressure exerted on the shoulder by fingers long since numbed. She tried to unwind her legs but could not. Mr. Cooke's body pinned her to the spot.

"Mr. Cooke," she whispered, "I have to move." In desperation she placed her hands in the middle of his bare back and rolled him forward. Quickly gathering her skirts, she twisted over him to the edge of the bed.

"Don't try to stand yet. You'll fall flat. Let me rub some blood back into your limbs first." And before Gabrielle had time to object, Doc had flipped up her skirts, pushed up her pantaloons, and proceeded to massage her legs vigorously. There was a determination in his actions which let her know he would brook no nonsense about modesty. Tightening her lips, she resolved to endure despite the rising color in her neck and face.

The men in the car coughed, cleared their throats, and cast their eyes elsewhere. All save Jordan Cooke.

Looking over her shoulder, she spoke to him, "You're certainly not a gentleman."

"You're absolutely right. Being a gentleman got me nowhere, so I gave it up." A wide smile imparted an elfin quality to his chiseled features, but the effect was wasted on Gabrielle.

Her back stiffened and her head pivoted forward. His voice, though weak, held an accent she had previously missed. He was a *Yankee!* She'd slaved, suffered, prayed for, and endured humiliation today to save a murdering, marauding *Yankee.* Hatred rose high in her throat and tasted bitter as bile on her tongue.

CHAPTER 2

"HERE'S SOME LAUDANUM when the morphine's gone and the pain comes bad."

Doc was talking to Gabrielle as though she was going to nurse this murderer. "I'll have nothing further to do with him," she announced in a muted voice turned icy with loathing.

"Finally figured out he was a Yankee, did you?" Doc cocked his head to one side and squinted at her. "Not the way a nurse or a Christian's supposed to behave." His eyes bore through her. "And I fancy you pride yourself on bein' both."

How she wanted to shout down the wily old man, to tell him to mind his own business. Tell him he knew nothing about Christian service. Tell him she hadn't asked to be a nurse, didn't want to remember the agony that man and his kind had caused. Tell him . . . But Gabrielle swallowed hard, gulped down the words she wanted to scream. Try as she would, though, she couldn't swallow the vile taste of the hatred she bore Jordan Cooke. It refused to go away. All she could see as she looked at him were the bodies of the men-children, some not yet fifteen, broken, torn beyond repair, dead before they had had a chance to live. Killed by him and his kind. She still lived with the nightmares, still heard their screams, their pleading, their dying. And still hated the men who'd done that to boys, and left her helpless to mend the damage.

"Well, sister. Look around. See anyone who can tend this man? Or do you think his dyin'll bring back the boys you lost? Or give you back your youth, the dances you missed, the boy friends, dead before they could court you, the husband and children you don't have?"

Her hands clenched into separate fists. "Shut up," she spat with a ferocity that frightened her. "Shut up!" And she knew that at that moment, had she a weapon, she would have killed him. The emotion rolled through her leaving her weak, trembling, and sick at her stomach. Unable to stand, she collapsed onto the bed. A groan let her know she had jarred Jordan Cooke badly. That sound returned her to sanity. *Oh, Lord, forgive me. Remove this unholy hatred that keeps my heart cold and now makes me want to kill.*

"I'm so sorry," she whispered to Mr. Cooke. "So very sorry," she kept repeating as she wiped her silent tears and stacked pillows behind his back to help steady him against the rocking jolting motion of the train.

Doc sprawled in the seat across the aisle, vacated for his benefit, and waited for her to regain her composure. At last she felt strong enough to face him, imagining that he could continue to accurately read her every thought.

"I owe you an apology," he began in a gruff growl.

"No, no. It's all right," she interrupted. He wasn't the sort to humble himself and, since he'd been right on every count, he owed her nothing. Rather, she owed him for opening wounds left to fester for too long. It would not be easy, but with the Lord's help, she would work on the healing, beginning now. "You were giving me instructions concerning medication for Mr. Cooke." She attempted an impersonal and professional tone to carry them back to safe ground.

"Laudanum on demand for a couple days—no more. Watch for fever. Bathe the dressings in carbolic acid but leave 'em on. Shouldn't need changin' for several days unless somethin' looks wrong. Watch for fever. But you know all this." He seemed to be trying as hard as she to wipe out the past moments.

"I don't know Mr. Cooke's destination," she said, "but I'm not going all the way to California."

"How many days?"

"Three, I think."

"That'll be time enough to know if he's gonna need a doctor again." He turned to the conductor who'd been keeping abreast of the situation. "When you puttin' me off?"

"No hurry. How about having lunch in Grand Island and taking an east-bound freight? Catch up on your sleep in the caboose and make your rounds when you get back to Omaha."

A laugh rumbled around inside Doc, but he succeeded in keeping it captive. "Much obliged, sir. Haven't had a day like this in years."

The conductor took Doc on a tour of the train and Gabrielle was left alone with the sleeping patient. Doc's departure acted as a signal to the people in the car to return to normal activity. Everyone had sat nearly silent during the surgery, talking briefly in whispers. Now while they visited aloud, the men lit their cigars and pipes as a release from the tension, and opened the windows wide to set the air in motion against the heat.

In spite of the pillows, Mr. Cooke, in unconscious self-protection, had rolled away from the edge of the bed. This left enough room for Gabrielle to sit beside him, using the seat back to lean against. She looked down at her feet stretched in front of her on the bed, unshod and exposed, but could think of no way to hide them. It was much too warm for a cover, she wouldn't think of putting shoes on a bed, and she absolutely refused to curl her legs under her again today. Only now were the painful prickling and cramping subsiding and normal feeling returning.

She crossed her ankles and pulled her skirts down as far as they would go. If the passengers in the car thought she was a loose woman, so be it. They weren't going to be her neighbors, and she could live with that judgment for three days. Looking around, however, she found no one seemed to be paying her the slightest attention. So much for thinking she was the center of attraction.

The drama was over. Mr. Cooke was sleeping peacefully, and so she allowed herself to relax for the first time in several hours. Each pair of facing seats had two windows and they provided both moving air and a grand view of the passing landscape. She could look out and see the Platte River, and there along its banks the deeply rutted trails of Conestoga wagons.

For years she had faithfully read the newspaper accounts of pioneer adventures and dreamed of someday making the trip. It had been her younger sister, however, who had answered an ad in the newspaper and gone West to marry a stranger, Edward Bailey. Though none of the family had yet met Mr. Bailey, Gabrielle had taken some comfort in the letters her sister wrote, assuring them that she was well and happy.

Now Edward Bailey was providing Gabrielle's escape from the drudgery of poverty and the bitter endlessness of unwanted spinsterhood. The good doctor knew when he spoke that the War had killed the men who would have courted her, married her, and given her children. The few Tennessee men left were captured by the charming, the beautiful, the well-to-do. Most certainly a blunt-spoken, plain, poorly paid nurse had no chance at all.

She reached out and touched Mr. Cooke's skin. It felt dry and cool and there was no stain on the dressing. Idly she let her thoughts drift as she watched him sleep. Was he married and a father? Somehow she didn't think so. He had an untamed look. She had seen it before in men who were still searching for something that yet eluded them. And because she kept just such a searching locked secretly deep inside herself, too, she recognized it in him.

Long, firm legs, the legs of a horseman, were drawn up to his chest. Perhaps he was too cool. She spread a sheet over him. The fists relaxed and he tucked one hand under his cheek. Recently barbered hair lay in sweat-stiff tawny streaks across his forehead. Again she had to fight the urge to smooth and straighten it. She had not seen the likes of him since she had nursed the soldiers. How had he remained free with so many eager eligible women longing for husbands? Why did he want to?

Her thoughts were getting out of hand and she braked them to a rapid halt. Reaching into the storage compartment at the head of the bed, she found her valise. She had paid good money for Crofutt's *Great Transcontinental Railroad Guide*, and she meant to use it. She had packed her travel valise according to Crofutt's instructions and been rewarded already by having a whisk broom handy when she had needed one. He also suggested wearing a lightweight summer suit upon leaving Omaha, with changes along the way. She would have to make do with the only one she possessed, a medium weight fabric in an autumn color. She flipped the pages until she found the description of the country they were passing through. She had only begun to read when her patient stirred.

"Water," he croaked and attempted to moisten his lips with a dry tongue.

"I'll be right back," she assured him and, taking a small metal cup from her bag, hurried to the washroom.

When she returned she found he had rolled onto his back as far as his injured shoulder would allow. She slipped her arm under his thick muscled neck and helped him rise onto his good arm. She held the cup while he drank in large thirsty gulps.

"More," he said in a more recognizable voice.

Again she filled the cup and again he emptied it.

"Thanks," he sighed and lay back down. The effort took its toll of his strength, and his skin again grew clammy and too cold. She took a blanket from the foot of the bed and covered him, plumping the pillows under his head. Now more comfortable, he lay watching her. She found the experience most unsettling.

Finally she could bear it no longer. "Please don't keep staring at me."

She ran a nervous hand over her hair which was parted in the middle and pulled into a bun at the back. A heavy mesh hairnet held it in place while traveling, but she could feel a few wispy strands which had escaped in the course of her morning's activities.

"If you're feeling better, I'd like to go to the washroom and freshen up," she said. It was a poor ploy, but served to give her an escape from the microscopic scrutiny of those penetrating eyes. After the scene with Doc, she felt emotionally transparent and still shaken enough to be vulnerable and defenseless. And, alas, she had had little early experience with worldly men and none in these last years. Her life centered on ill children and the infirm aged.

"I'm not feeling better," he admitted, "but my problem isn't something you can solve."

"Why not?" She wondered if he were going to be modest about having to use the bathroom. She didn't plan to attend him, but there were strong men among the passengers who could do so were she to ask.

27

"Happen to have a ham sandwich in your pocket?"
His grin turned squint marks into laugh lines and
revealed straight square teeth, white and well cared
for.

This time Gabrielle noticed every nuance of the
transformation from mature man to mischievous boy
and it totally disarmed her. That is, until she looked
carefully into his eyes. They didn't change. They held
no luster, no twinkle of mirth. *So, he hadn't been
allowed to kill and come away unscathed, after all.*

"Are you always so serious?" he asked.

She permitted herself a grim half-smile. "I'm afraid
so. In my work there isn't a lot of gaity."

"You mean you really are a nurse? I thought you
were someone's level-headed mother accustomed to
dealing with the emergencies of childhood." The look
on his chameleon-like face changed again. Now it
showed respect and a tiny cock in the eyebrow hinted
at a bit of curiosity.

"Oh, I deal with childhood emergencies all right.
Those the mothers can't face or can't help. Just once
I'd like to nurse a beginning spring cold or a simple
stomachache from too many green apples instead of
pneumonia or an appendix." Why was she babbling to
this man? He wasn't a father, and he probably
detested children.

"If not somebody's mother, surely somebody's
wife."

"No," she said abruptly. "Please excuse me while
I comb my hair." She picked up her small bag and
hurried down the aisle. If she took her time, perhaps
he would be asleep when she returned.

How she longed for the skills of flirtation, the ability
to sidestep the questions she didn't wish to answer in
a light, humorous manner. She had watched and
listened and even practiced cunning little answers in
private. But when she came face to face with a
situation, all those clever things she had imagined

slipped away and her words came out like lead, hard and heavy. Except with children. She could play and talk with them for hours in their make-believe worlds and feel light and easy. What was her problem? *Never grew up, I guess.*

With her face washed and her hair smoothed, she felt and looked more her normal self. Gathering her things and taking a deep breath, she stepped into the aisle. She even managed a smile for the men who had watched her every motion, even seen her pinch her cheeks to bring up a bit of color. What one couldn't change, one lived with until one could change it, had been her code for many years, and she could do nothing about the curtainless washroom. However, she was sure the men would soon tire of seeing the same people doing the same things over and over and, by their lack of interest, afford everyone some privacy.

Turning to make her way down the aisle, she hesitated. There, sitting on Mr. Cooke's bed with her skirts spread in a most picturesque manner, was Gabrielle's "angel" from the station platform in Omaha. While Mr. Cooke looked much better, he was still far from being out of danger. She took a deep breath and set her jaw. She was very experienced at dealing with unwanted visitors and also wanted ones. She marched up the aisle. "Excuse me, but Mr. Cooke is not yet well enough to have company." Her tone, cool and commanding, only drew a quizzical look from the lady.

"Nurse, this is an old friend and foe, Melanie DeWitt." Jordan introduced them but never took his eyes from his beautiful visitor.

"We met earlier." She gave a toss of her light ash blond ringlets, fashionably pulled back from her face and cascading down the back of her head to her shoulders. "But we haven't been formally introduced. How do you do, Nurse." Her voice was gold velvet over-sewn with a thick Southern drawl.

"The name is Miss Gabrielle Sevier," she said evenly, her height allowing her to reach easily over Miss DeWitt to return her toilette articles to the storage compartment.

"Well, Miss Sevier, did you find a ham sandwich while you were gone?"

"Unfortunately, there seems to be none aboard. However, I understand we will be stopping shortly for lunch. At that time, I shall see what I can locate. In the meantime, Miss DeWitt, there is very little room here, and I would appreciate it if you would wait until later to visit with Mr. Cooke."

Melanie DeWitt drew her mouth into an attractive little pout. "Jordan doesn't seem to be minding."

"Mr. Cooke doesn't know what's good for him at present. He may have visitors later." Gabrielle held her voice and look steady.

"Do I really have to go?" she asked of Jordan.

"She's the nurse, and I've never had the courage to argue with one." He was putting up a good front, but the timbre in his voice was getting noticeably weaker.

Miss DeWitt gathered her skirts and, giving him a dazzling smile to remember her by, returned to her seat. She also left a lingering scent of lilacs. *And I leave carbolic acid,* Gabrielle thought.

Returning from the tour, Doc stood looking down at his patient. "You're lookin' a mite whey-faced. Been tryin' to prove you're a tough buzzard 'fore you're ready," he observed, his naturally sour expression firmly in place.

"Can't prove anything on an empty stomach," Jordan retorted, weakly.

"Well, lick your chops and start salivatin'. Grand Island's the next stop and you can eat. When am I gonna see you to take out them stitches?"

"I'll be east again in a couple of weeks. I'll stop in your office then."

"Timin's good. Here's my card. Ask for my office if

you don't know Omaha." He handed Jordan a smudged dog-eared business card.

"About the fee . . . you can pay your bill when I see you. I'm frettin' about the lady, here. She's a professional and as such, deserves your money same as I do."

Gabrielle started to object, but Doc held up his hand to silence her. She reacted automatically to years of obeying the doctors' commands, and so her objections remained unvoiced.

"I plan to pay her. Would you like to see me do it?"

"No. I trust your word."

Turning to Gabrielle, he took her hand and clasped it in both of his. "If you ever need work or a reference, count on me. You're one h . . . fine nurse. Be proud to have you at my side any time."

"Thank you, Doctor. You're a very fine surgeon, and it would be a privilege to work with you. Goodbye, and enjoy your trip back to Omaha." She helped him check his bag and then watched as he left. A slight shuffle and shoulders beginning to stoop told of the years of service he'd given with too little thought for himself.

The train slowed and people began jumping off before it was well stopped. "I suggest you forget being a lady and make for the food. We only stop for a half hour and that's not long with a mob this big to feed." Mr. Cooke was looking out the window at the stream of hungry passengers filing into the station. "Get some money out of my pocket. Don't let 'em charge you more'n a dollar."

She did as she was bidden and hurried into the dining room. He was right. The place was packed with people screaming their orders and elbowing their way to the tables. It was insane. She looked at a plate being set on the table . . . the meat looked carved from a boot, sweet potatoes, undercooked she suspected, boiled Indian corn with hoecakes, and every-

31

thing floating in grease and syrup. She'd never seen such unappetizing food in her life. The wound hadn't killed her patient, but she was sure he would not survive this. Putting on her best no-nonsense face, she marched through the dining room and into the kitchen. It was a madhouse and no one even noticed her. She ducked waiters laden with heavy trays and dodged flying butcher knives until she found a clean dinner plate. Grabbing a fork, she found a pan of meat still cooking on the stove. She speared a piece before it could be incinerated, tested the boiling potatoes until she found one well-cooked, spotted some loaves of fresh-baked bread, cut a large still-warm slice and buttered both it and the potato. There was a pot of stew simmering on the back of the stove and she helped herself to a bowlful.

"What do you think you're doing?" a voice roared at her.

Taking a deep breath and praying for courage, she turned to stare into a beet red face with popping eyes, and a mouth from which projected a long-dead, well-chewed cigar. "I have a very sick patient aboard the train and I am preparing a special plate. If you doubt my word, you are free to check with the doctor who has tended him from Omaha. He's eating in your dining room this minute." Gabrielle swept up the bowl and plate, glided past the cook, and became lost in the mob before he could collect himself and stop her.

Climbing aboard the train with both hands full proved difficult. Opening the heavy door into the car, however, was impossible. She had no choice but to wait until someone came along. Fortunately, she didn't wait long, and she was able to set still steaming food in front of her patient.

"What miracle did you perform? This is the first food I've seen at this station that looked palatable."

"Never mind. Lie still and I'll feed you the stew first."

"Feed me! I don't need feeding. I learned to use a knife and fork years ago."

"All right, if you insist." She stepped back and rested against the seat across the aisle. He grabbed a spoon in his left hand and dived into the stew. All he came up with was gravy. After several unsuccessful attempts to cut the large pieces of carrot and potato, he sheepishly asked her to help him. He was still eating hungrily as the train left the station, commenting between nearly every bite on how amazingly good everything tasted.

"I'm not sure how good you'll think it is when I tell you I forgot to pay for it."

His impish grin lighted his face. "I'll pay when I come this way next time."

"And return their dishes."

"Absolutely not! Do you think I'm carting these things across half a continent? Throw them out. I'll pay for them, too." He picked up the dishes and cutlery and sent them sailing through the open window.

After lunch, a new distraction was added to the car. Several people had purchased box lunches in Omaha or brought their own, and now the bouquet from them hung heavy in the air. The flies, smelling a feast, descended in swarms.

Gabrielle made a fan from a discarded newspaper and tried to keep them off Mr. Cooke as he slept. She let her eyes roam over the passengers as she sat beside him. Miss DeWitt had vanished shortly after Gabrielle dismissed her and had not returned. People sat twisted into various contortions as they tried to make themselves comfortable. Apparently the small couch-like benches that made into beds weren't as comfortable as they looked.

They still traveled beside the Platte River and the pioneer trail. Occasionally now she saw the bleached bones of long-dead oxen and horses beside the deep ruts carved by crawling covered wagons. A solitary grave marker, a broken wheel, a piece of discarded furniture, too dear to leave at first, marked their passing.

Finally Mr. Cooke slept so deeply he seemed not to notice the flies and, at the next stop, Gabrielle stepped off the train for a short, brisk walk. She could never have imagined any land so immense. It seemed to stretch to the edge of the world and beyond in every direction. The constant whispering wind carried the pungent smell of hay, dust, and cattle, mixed with the fragrance of dried spices. The endless sea of monotonous grayish-green grass undulated in gentle wavelike motion. Gray buffalo grass, once eaten by buffalo now exterminated save for a few small herds, and whitish-yellow prairie grass fed the mottled cattle standing immobile in the heat. In the distance cowboys wearing cream-white hats and riding lanky ponies, guarded the stock. A warning whistle seemed to bound back from the silent, soft sea of grass and bring with it the unexplainable passive sadness resting there. Gabrielle shook herself from the trance and climbed quickly onto the train.

Jordan Cooke was awake when she returned. "Enjoying the scenery?"

"Yes. There is surely a great deal of it to enjoy. I never imagined anything like it."

"It's not called the Great Plains for nothing," he reminded her.

"But it gives a new dimension to the word *great*, doesn't it?"

"Come, sit back and rest." He reached and placed pillows behind her back. "At the next stop, I want you awake."

"Why?" she asked and relaxed her body against the enfolding cushions.

"You'll see," was all he would say.

The braking of the train jarred her awake, and she opened her eyes to find him watching her. "Are you ready for your first Indian warriors?"

"On the train?" she choked.

"No. Look outside." His eyes never left her face as he waited for her reaction.

There standing at the side of the car was a warrior, his face wildly painted. He flaunted a war bonnet from which trailed many feathers far down his back. The blanket wrapped around him was festooned with dried scalps blowing in the wind. Her hand flew to her mouth to stifle a scream. "Mr. Cooke, is it safe?"

His low rolling laugh told her she had reacted the way he had hoped. "The Pawnees abandoned their horse-buffalo culture and the white man moved them onto a reservation two years ago. Now they put on a show and live off what they cadge from the sight-seers."

Was this part of the oppressive mysterious sadness of the land she had felt earlier? The Confederacy wasn't the only country destroyed on this continent. How many Indian nations were reduced to begging? She felt the knot in her heart which had begun to soften, again tie itself tight and hard. It wasn't a comfortable feeling, but it was familiar.

He slept again and she fanned the flies. As the train slowed for one of its numerous stops that afternoon, she could see the prairie-dog villages promised in her guidebook. Little rodents sunned near the entrances to their burrows, built dangerously close to the tracks. They played like children, flinging themselves into the air with happy abandon, flipping numerous somersaults before presenting two golden furry heels and a short furry tail and disappearing into the tunnels to their underground homes. She almost laughed aloud at the sight and some of her melancholy dissipated.

"Sidney, Nebraska," the conductor called through the car. "Supper stop."

"This place specializes in antelope steak, and it's pretty good if it's not over-cooked," Jordan said in a sleepy voice.

She again tested his forehead. He remained cool and the bandage clean. He was making a remarkable recovery. "You are one continuous appetite," she said smiling.

"Especially when I skip two meals."

"What two meals? I fed you dinner."

"But you weren't around to take care of me last night for supper or see that I had breakfast," he retorted.

"I didn't come on duty until after the breakfast hour, but you don't remember much about that." She was actually bantering with him, holding her own, and enjoying it immensely.

The train jerked to a stop, and she sprinted toward the dining room. He was right. This was worse. The food was already on the table and the flies were finishing their first course. She bolted into the kitchen, grabbed the nearest plate and proceeded to fill it with what she presumed to be antelope steak and fried potatoes from the containers on the stove. Here, at least, the flies felt less at home. She moved in and out so quickly that the startled cooks did no more than gape. She snatched eating utensils from one of the tables as she whirled past.

"I've never seen so many flies," she said as she began cutting the meat. She had rescued the steak before it could be overcooked and it smelled delicious. She hadn't eaten since very early this morning and her mouth began to water as the delectable odors rose from the plate in front of her. "I do believe the flies from Grand Island telegraphed their friends and relatives and had them meet in Sidney for supper." Maybe if she thought about the flies hard enough, she would lose her appetite.

"Looks like I'm going to be this way for awhile and

I won't always have you. I'd like to practice feeding myself."

She handed him the fork and held the plate so he wouldn't have so far to balance the food. There was little conversation as he concentrated on the normally routine act made unpleasantly difficult and awkward. Suddenly, the fork paused in midair. "You haven't eaten all day. Eat," he commanded.

She shook her head. "You need the nourishment if you're to get well, Mr. Cooke."

"Pick up that spoon and eat," he ordered, "or I'll forcefeed you."

She loathed being ordered about even when the intentions were the best. She was very tempted to set his plate down and seek other company.

Apparently he sensed her hostility. "Please," he added softly and handed her the spoon. "And please, call me Jordan. Mr. Cooke's my father."

It didn't sit well, calling a patient by his first name, but she had learned enough about Jordan Cooke to know he would insist and probably rather violently. "Very well, Jordan."

"That's much better." And they ate the rest of the meal in silence.

She and Jordan relaxed after supper and gazed idly at the gathering black clouds. He raised his hand and gestured toward the window. "Watch," he said and then let the hand fall carelessly across hers as it lay half-open by her side.

Should she say something? Perhaps move her hand away? Without turning her head, she observed him from the corner of her eye. He seemed oblivious of his act, for the hand remained motionless and his attention remained fixed on the passing scene.

A great bolt of lightning flashed, connecting sky to earth for a brief second. It seemed a signal, and the bolts flashed in every direction and huge balls of electric fire rolled over the plains.

"Has the artillery of heaven made us a target? Are we doomed to instant destruction?"

Though asked in an almost inaudible voice with no answer expected, his questions stunned her. Perhaps she had judged him too hastily. Maybe he was not what he appeared.

It began raining with such force that the landscape disappeared behind a watery curtain. The train slowed, and the porter came through to light the lamps in a futile effort to dispel the premature darkness.

About the time Gabrielle decided God's promise had been forgotten, the deluge stopped. There, set against the forbidding black clouds, arched a brilliant rainbow. She smiled and looked at Jordan. A faint wistfulness shadowed the impassive planes of his face. It lingered briefly, then was gone, leaving no visible trace of its existence.

CHAPTER 3

THEY PASSED THROUGH THE STORM and the sun, low on the horizon, streamed through the windows and lit the inside of the car. The light from the oil lamps became insignificant beside its glory. As Jordan looked out the window, Gabrielle found herself again assessing him. In her heart of hearts, she wanted to know more about him, ask about his past, but that would never do. One never became that familiar with a patient and that was all he was, she reminded herself. As she looked down at his hand still protecting hers, however, she had difficulty convincing herself.

His color was better, and his face in a different light revealed what the sharp-eyed doctor had seen earlier. A faint, thin line of white ran from his temple and ended at the jaw line. She fought the urge to reach out and soothe the scar, as though her touch would banish it and the memory of how it was acquired. He turned his eyes quickly, seeming to feel her gaze upon him, and their eyes met. His eyes were a softer green than she remembered, with tiny flecks of gold floating in their depths. To her consternation she felt her neck and face grow hot and knew she was blushing. Was that a glint of amusement she saw lighting the green depths?

"Well, well. What guilty thoughts did I interrupt?" he taunted.

Please, Lord, let me keep my voice calm. Everything else has fallen apart. "I hadn't noticed the scar on your cheek and was wondering how you acquired it." How cool and impersonal she sounded. Her prayer had been answered and, with it, a return of her senses.

His face grew hard and brittle. The gold flecks disappeared and the eyes narrowed. All tenderness fled as he rubbed the tiny ridge with the fingers of his left hand, and while he said nothing, she sensed a turmoil churning through him far larger than the narrow scar. Then he raked his fingers through his hair. "This stuff isn't hair, it's straw. There's a comb in my bag." He ignored her inquiry as though it had never been spoken.

Gabrielle, making a large mental note not to forget the nurse-patient relationship again, searched the storage compartment. There, stuffed in a corner was a small black leather satchel which carried his shaving materials and a few other things, including the comb. "Lie back and I'll see about making you presentable." She looked up from the satchel in time to see Melanie DeWitt return to the car. "I see visiting hours are about to begin." Gabrielle spoke in a matter-of-fact tone, making sure her voice held nothing he could respond to.

He snatched the comb from her hand and made a swipe through his hair. The comb stuck in the sweaty strands, and his shoulder sagged in defeat.

"I may not get it just as you want, but I do have two hands and, as dirty as your hair is, it's going to take both of them to comb it."

"Wash it! I hate dirty hair!"

There he was, ordering her about again. She would have liked arguing it out, but since she had only two more days of his boorishness, it wasn't worth the bother. "You're not strong enough for a thorough shampoo, and there isn't any cornmeal to give you a dry cleansing. I'll do the best I can with a wet wash cloth." She rose from the bed and started down the aisle to fill the basin.

"Is it visiting hours, yet?" Miss DeWitt asked as Gabrielle passed.

"I'm in the process of preparing the patient for the pleasure of your company. When we've finished getting some of the muck out of his hair, I think he'll be ready to receive you." She flashed a no-mirth smile at the lovely lady sitting so cool and elegant.

While Gabrielle was waiting for the basin to fill, she studied herself in the mirror, making the comparison with Melanie DeWitt. Plain brown hair. Oval face with two lines already forming between plain brown eyes. Slight pouches under the eyes, creases at the corners. A long nose that flared a bit at the nostrils and a wide mouth with full lips. A forced smile revealed too many teeth, but—miracle—all were straight and white, even though they were large and square. Clear smooth skin, firm chin, but if she ever gained an ounce of weight, it would all go under her chin, a tendency inherited from her mother.

She wondered if Mr. Bailey would be absolutely horrified when he saw her. He had seemed such a nice man in his letters, and Ellen had loved him. But she and Ellen didn't look anything alike, a fact Gabrielle had repeatedly mentioned in her letters.

Well, Miss DeWitt, with your curls, heart-shaped face and cupid's bow mouth that shows the proper amount of tiny even teeth when you smile, I don't plan to give you any competition for Mr. Cooke's attentions. You can have him all to yourself. She carried the deep bowl back to the bed, spread the oilcloth

41

cover and banked towels around Jordan's neck. "It's particularly dirty where you fell. Let's work on that spot first." Sitting on the bed beside him, she took strands of hair between folds of the wet cloth. After several trips for clean water, she managed to remove most of the dirt. At last she could get the comb through his hair.

"Never having seen you with your hair combed, you'll have to direct me."

"There's a mirror in my bag." She found it and handed it to him. "Part it on the left, just off center."

The thick wet hair parted with some difficulty, but she managed not to scalp him.

"How tall are you anyway?" he asked as she completed the chore.

"Five feet, nine inches." She always felt gargantuan since that was the height of most men and few women.

"Everyone in your family tall?" He kept trying to talk as she washed him and the words came out distorted.

"No. Just me. My father says I'm a throw-back to the Vikings and their warrior women."

"And what do you say?"

"I say it's because I'm always so curious and constantly stretching to see what's going on."

"I like your father's version better. You'd look right at home in a helmet with horns and a shield and spear."

He gave her a wicked look, and waited for her to rise to the bait. *Well, he'll wait a long time.* "There, I think you're ready to receive Miss DeWitt if she isn't offended by a bare, hairy chest. I'd rather not put anything over that shoulder just yet."

"And I'd rather you didn't. If she's offended, we can always draw the bed curtain, and she can leave."

In spite of herself, Gabrielle blushed again. What was it about this man that caused her to react in such an emotionally irresponsible manner? He laughed and she hurried to clean up the mess. She smoothed his sheet and re-folded the blanket since the train had moved on past the coolness of the storm, and they were again into dust and flies. She walked back to empty the water. "All ready, Miss DeWitt. Mr. Cooke's expecting you."

Gabrielle sat in Miss DeWitt's seat, but she couldn't keep her eyes from Jordan, laughing and talking with his guest. Her reactions of jealousy and envy were new to Gabrielle. Since first-class passengers had complete freedom of the train, she decided to escape by exercising her privilege.

Stepping out the door, she encountered a blast of hot air, dust, and cinders, which made her think twice about venturing farther. Then she thought about the alternative and tugged open the door leading to the next car. It was a Pullman, a duplicate of the one in which she was riding. However, the aisle was blocked by the train's newsboy making his everlasting rounds. Up to now, she'd been too busy to be much aware of him. Interested, she paused in the washroom door and watched the boy of perhaps fourteen or even younger, peddling his wares—candy, peanuts, cigars, yesterday's newspapers, magazines, and dirty dime novels for all he could get for them among the bored and restless passengers.

He pulled a copy of *Velvet Vice* from under the stack of Police Gazettes and sold it to a red-faced little man who immediately slid it under his coat. A large busy woman came tromping back from the "convenience" and plunked down in the seat opposite him. Gabrielle wondered when he would be able to sneak away to read his spicy book.

The boy came to stand in front of her. "You ain't bought nothin' the whole trip," he accused.

"As you have undoubtedly noticed, as you've made your continual rounds, I have been extremely busy nursing the gentleman in the other car."

"You ain't now, though." He stood, practically daring her not to give him some business.

She wondered what he would do if she didn't. She fingered the items in his tray. "How'd you get this job?"

"Railroad gives me permission. I buy my own stuff, and I get one round trip a week, Omaha to Ogden and back."

"Why just to Ogden?"

"Central Pacific takes over there. You get different cars, new crew, and another butch. You gonna buy somethin', lady? I got a big train to cover."

Gabrielle decided on a small sack of peanuts. These would be nourishing in case the food became completely inedible.

"Thanks. Take good care of the big guy. He's a big spender when's he's feeling good. But watch out for the lady," the little fellow warned.

"Why?" Gabrielle asked, startled at his warning.

"She's a cardsharp. Travels the road real regular. Her and him plays a lotta high-stake poker when they make the same run and she pulls out her railroad bible." He started to leave.

"Wait. I don't understand your expression, 'railroad bible.'"

He looked at her with high disgust. "Cards, lady. A deck of cards. You plannin' to buy something else?"

His practiced little eyes pinned on her face made her feel guilty for having detained him without making a further purchase. "Uh, yes. I'll take two mints, please."

He allowed her to choose her candies, then without further communication, pocketed the money, adroitly swung his tray through the heavy door, and disappeared.

She placed the mints in with the peanuts, dropped the sack into her duster pocket, and made her way through the car, and into the first of the day coaches.

Here the short-haul and less affluent travelers sat or tried to sleep on upholstered seats less comfortable than the ones in her Pullman. The air was heavily laden with tobacco smoke, and the smell of box lunches and unwashed bodies. The passengers were not the elegant, carefully dressed gentlemen in first class, but bearded, mustached cowhands, miners, farmers, and hunters dressed in a variety of stained clothing and carrying their personal items wrapped in dirty bundles. She noticed many of them had revolvers stuck in their belts. The talk was loud and boisterous and liberally laced with profanity. She stared at several Indians, faces immobile, curled into wretched blankets. If this was the real West, and she had a feeling it was, she wondered if she was prepared for it. She clung to the fact that Ellen had loved it, and tried not to think that it had also killed her. Giving silent thanks to Mr. Bailey for insisting she travel in the Pullman Palace car, Gabrielle bolstered her courage and continued on into the third class.

The car was built like a long, narrow wooden box and fitted with two rows of wooden benches stretching on either side of a narrow aisle. And here rode the immigrant people she had watched in Omaha. The air, even more heavily laden with tobacco smoke, lingering food odors, and the sour smell of body odor nearly suffocated her. Hard wooden seat backs pivoted to swing either way and, by placing a rented board between the benches and covering it with three square pillows stuffed with straw, a crude bed could be contrived. Small oil lamps glimmered at intervals along the dingy unpainted walls giving only feeble illumination. At the far end from where she stood, a wooden stove provided warmth in the winter and a place to cook. Gabrielle stood next to the enclosed space reserved for the toilet, or "convenience," and watched a man fill a wash basin from the water filter opposite the stove. Then, while a chum held the door open, he went out onto the platform between the moving cars, knelt down, hung on with one elbow crooked around the railing, and made a cold, dangerous toilet.

The train slowed for another of its nearly two hundred and thirty stops before San Francisco. As Gabrielle watched, a family—mother, father, three nearly grown sons, and two young daughters—gathered their meager belongings and stepped out into the night. There was no town. "What are they going to do?" Gabrielle asked a woman sitting stony faced on a torturous bench.

She shrugged and pointed. Gabrielle turned. "I speak a little English," a gangly boy said.

"They're getting off in the middle of nowhere. I only see a building that looks something like a train station. What will they do?"

"Building is railroad's. People stay there while they find land and build house."

Gabrielle slumped down onto the recently vacated, hard, incredibly narrow bench while she tried to absorb what she had been told. She didn't doubt his words, she just couldn't imagine people with such faith. Faith enough to leave everything, travel thousands of miles in the most dehumanizing conditions, and arrive at their dream to find a drafty, dusty shack in a desolate land.

She was visibly shaken. She had thought she was being terribly brave, making her trek into the unknown, but she was on an excursion by comparison. "Thank you," she said. "Where are you going?"

"West," was his answer, and he stared straight ahead, ignoring her.

When would she learn to stop asking questions? People out here told you what they wanted you to know, and no more, and took offense at any sign of prying. She smiled at him and excused herself. It was time she put an end to Jordan's visiting hour and started preparing him for the night.

46

Upon returning, she dismissed Miss DeWitt, who Gabrielle noted, had had the good sense not to produce her 'railroad bible.' Apparently she had realized Mr. Cooke was in no condition to play poker tonight.

Gabrielle proceeded to tear an extra sheet longways into strips about three inches wide. The ripping noise startled the passengers but she made no explanation, only continued until the entire sheet was in bandages.

"What are you planning to do?" Jordan finally asked.

"Get you ready for the night," she said. "Bend your elbow and lay your arm across your stomach. You'll have to support it with your other hand." She arranged the injured arm. "Sit up." Two could play at this command business. Starting at the top of the shoulder, she began to wrap the strips around him, securing his arm to his body.

"You're turning me into a mummy," he objected.

"Think how profitable it could be. We could take you to out-of-the-way places and sell tickets to let the people see you. Make you rich in no time." She continued until his arm above the elbow was firmly bound. Then, she took a large square and folded it into a triangle.

"Seems you're making a big thing of going to bed."

"I am. Have to earn my money." She gently took the arm he was holding and placed it in the triangle. "This sling will support your arm and help keep your shoulder immobile while you sleep. And I presume you might want to do more than lounge in bed all day tomorrow. In short, it should make you more comfortable."

"Well, it doesn't. Take it off!"

"You will leave the wrapping exactly as I have finished it. If you move to change it, I shall leave you to fare the best you can for the remainder of the trip."

"Not an idle threat?"

"Most certainly not."

"I didn't think so."

Turning to the two men across the aisle, she asked, "Will you two gentlemen be so good as to help Mr. Cooke to the "convenience" again. With his arm supported, it will be less of a chore." She stepped out of the way, and the men rose to assist Jordan.

"I don't want help. I can get there myself." He dropped his legs over the edge of the bed and moved to stand. The train gave an unexpected lurch and had not the two men held him, his injured shoulder would have been thrown against the back of a seat.

"Still think you don't need help?"

He said nothing, but the glare he sent her way was sufficient to do her in had she been made of less stern stuff. While he was away she prepared his bed for a sponge bath, laying out a protective oil cloth and towels, and filling the basin with warm water.

As he rolled into the re-made bed, she noticed small beads of sweat forming on his forehead and upper lip. "Thank you, sirs. I greatly appreciate your assistance even if he doesn't."

"Uh, thanks," he said, following her prompting.

While the porters made up the beds for the night, the passengers stood in lines at the washroom. Gabrielle carefully balanced the water and prayed the train would track steady for a few minutes. A lurch like the last one would drown Jordan's bed, and he would become even more difficult to deal with.

Jordan lay back and she pulled the bed curtain, affording him some privacy for his bath. "I'm not having a bath."

She stood staring down at him. Why was he acting like a spoiled brat? She really didn't feel like teasing him into accepting the washing as she would have a child. Then she noticed the muscles in his jaw working behind the clamped lips. "Why didn't you tell me you were hurting?" Remembering it had been several hours since his last dose, she spooned some laudanum down him. Gently she set about to wash a section at a time. She washed the pale face, now a whiskery stubble field. Next she lightly soaped his good arm and shoulder, rinsed it and wiped it dry. Then, she took the wet cloth and wiped over the mid-section left exposed. Taking a box of talc from her valise, she sprinkled some in her hand and gave him a back rub. She felt him relax and settle down against the pillows. She emptied the water, put away the protective cloth, and came to sit with him until he slept.

"Gabby, you can tuck me in every night," he murmured.

He had struck a nerve this time. How she detested that nickname! She wanted to tell him not to call her Gabby, but he looked too near asleep, and she didn't want to rouse him. Time enough if he called her that again. Wearily, she deposited her valise in the top berth, and climbed the ladder.

The area was anything but spacious. The bed curtain was long and served both the upper and lower berth. She pulled them together only to find that then they didn't cover the ends. She left the middle closed and choosing not to dangle her legs into the aisle, sat cross-legged. As she unfastened and removed her blouse, she wished desperately some kind soul would give her a sponge bath. Removing her skirt and hanging it over the railing, she sat now in her underthings wondering just how much she should undress. If she had to tend Jordan in the night, she didn't want to be immodestly unclad, yet it was uncomfortably warm up against the ceiling. She decided to lay out her robe and sleep as she was. Loosening her camisole, she pulled it out of her petticoat.

Her hair fell to its full length down her back as she removed the hair net and pins. No matter how tired she was, she never failed to give it a good brushing, and tonight was no exception. She took her mind from her weariness and the tedium of the nightly brushing by reviewing what she knew about Miss DeWitt. What was her background that she would waste her beauty and brains traveling across the country, making her way as a professional gambler? Gabrielle remembered skimming the warning in Mr. Crofutt's guidebook against gambling with cards should someone you didn't know offer to entertain you. But since she didn't plan to become involved, she gave it scant attention. Tomorrow she would re-read that page.

Tying a ribbon around her head to keep the shiny hair from her eyes while she slept, she lay back on the pillow and stretched out. To take advantage of what little air there was, she pulled up her camisole to expose the skin of her stomach, and raised the petticoat to let the air move across her legs below the pantaloons.

Relaxing, she let her eyes wander across the beautifully polished panels of wood overhead. She blinked and looked again. There above her was Jordan's face, a crooked grin cocked on one side. The highly polished wood acted as a mirror and he had watched her every move. She leaned over the edge and looked down into his berth. "You are an insufferable man! How could you lie there and watch and not say anything?" She put on her robe and threw herself back onto her pillow.

He answered with a soft, deep chuckle.

CHAPTER 4

GABRIELLE OPENED HER EYES. She lay, groggy and disoriented, sure of only one thing—a soft, shifting weight about her head that told her all was not well. In the dark she could see nothing, so without moving anything else, she slowly raised an exploratory hand and touched the object keeping her pinned to her pillow. It felt a bit cool and slightly hairy, and at her touch, moved against her face. There was a distinct odor about it, a mixture of dirt and sweat. She wanted to scream and only by exerting the greatest self-control did she keep her rising terror mute.

Further cautious examination revealed that it connected to the berth behind hers. What kind of terrible western animal had crawled into both berths? Moving her fingertips down the hairy length and back toward her head, she found the hair becoming thinner. She must be getting close to its head, and her heart nearly leaped from her chest knowing the creature's head lay next to her face. *What would it do to her if she touched it on the eye or nose. Or worse, the mouth?* She could end up with missing fingers, a disfiguring bite on her cheek. . . . She refused to think further.

51

It lay across her hair and she could not move her upper body. What should she do? It was so dark and the sounds of heavy regular breathing and snoring let her know that most of the car was still in deep sleep.

But she had to do something. It moved again on the other side of her. Were there two of them? God forbid. She lifted the other hand and placed trembling fingers along a similar form on that side of her head. She also felt less hair on that one the closer she came to her head. Now she fingered a bony lump. *Was that its nose?* If it was, that meant she was dangerously close to the mouth. Keeping her fingertip contact with the intruder, she continued to move slowly along toward the mouth. It moved! She jerked and a tiny scream escaped against her will.

"What's the matter?" Jordan asked in a whisper. *Oh, heavens.* She had wakened him. "N-n-nothing," she lied. The thing moved again, and she could not control the quivering cry that told of her fright.

The bed below rustled and groaned as Jordan struggled to stand. Then, she was aware of a muffled but deep, rolling laugh. *The Beast! How could he?* But if she was in danger, he surely wouldn't stand there laughing. Would he? The creature was suddenly gone and its twin with it. She was free! Still nearly immobile from fright, she turned her eyes to see a convulsing Jordan, a sheet stuffed in his mouth and tears rolling down his face, pointing toward where the creatures had emerged. She raised up and looked. There, curled together, the soles of two very large feet hooked to two well-muscled, extremely hairy legs disappeared back into the neighboring berth. Relief surged through her, and burying her face in her pillow, she joined him in laughter.

Each time the laughter started to subside, they would look at each other, and it would rise like a fountain and flow again. How she longed to throw back her head and let the mirth have full release, but there might accidentally be someone still asleep, though she doubted it. Just then the porter came through with his first wake-up call. That was all she and Jordan needed. They collapsed into gales of laughter, and she only stopped when her sides ached too badly to continue.

"That was one of the funniest things I have ever seen," Jordan gasped as he tried to regain his composure. "I shall have a glorious time telling about it for the rest of my life."

Wiping the tears from her cheeks, she had to agree with him. "But I don't remember many times when I was more terrified," she confessed.

Remembering he was her patient, she quickly asked, "How are you feeling this morning?"

"Until a minute ago, like I'd been run over by this train, rather than riding on it."

"You didn't sleep?"

"Only until the laudanum wore off. That was a pretty healthy slug you gave me."

"Sounds like you need some more."

"I'm fine. I don't want any more. I want some food. I've never eaten so well on a train trip."

As if hearing Jordan's remark, the news butch entered the car, shouting at the top of his little lungs, "Breakfast in Cheyenne in forty-five minutes!"

"How is the food?" a dainty voice called from behind one of the curtained bedrooms.

"Ma'am, I'd like to say it was good, but it's not to my taste. You may find it just fine," the butch answered.

A loud chorus of moans greeted the news. "And we can't even stay in bed and nurse our abused stomachs," another groaned.

"It gets worse the further west we go," Jordan said.

"What good news. I can hardly wait to see worse if what we've had is better. And you'd best stand out of the aisle before you get trampled," she advised Jordan. "That's not much time for twenty-nine people to use the facilities."

He sank from sight and she sat up. She started to remove her robe and then remembered last night. Looking at the ceiling, she saw his reflection, but this morning the eyes were shut and the mouth drawn tight. The small muscles in his jaw were working again, his way of coping with pain. There was no need for him to suffer like that. Why had he refused the drug?

She dressed as quickly as the cramped quarters allowed, brushed her hair, and coiled it into a chignon on the back of her head. After replacing the mesh net, she slipped on her duster and repacked her valise. She climbed down the ladder, but with the bed still made up, there wasn't a great deal of room and so she stowed it under the lower berth. She'd put it in the storage compartment later.

"Lady, mind moving?"

"Sorry." The aisles were so narrow that there wasn't room for two people to pass. She tumbled through the curtains onto Jordan's bed. He opened opaque jade eyes and looked dully at her. She tested his forehead. It was a bit hot, and she felt a quick knot tie in her stomach. "I wish you'd let me give you something for the pain," she begged.

"Not taking any more stuff." Even though his voice was weak, there was a timbre running in it that told her not to argue.

"If you can stand it, I'd like to unwrap your arm and check the dressings on the wound."

"Go ahead." She could see and feel him steel himself against the coming torture.

Please God, help me to be gentle and let me not find infection. She unfastened the sling supporting his arm and undid the wrapping. By rolling the strips of sheet as she went, she was able to unbind him without

54

moving him too much. He felt warm when he should have felt cool and the closer she got to the bandage itself, the more apprehensive she became. She had little to treat him with if a problem was developing; and, if the food and dining rooms were getting more and more primitive, she could only imagine what the medical service must be like.

At last she was down to the dressing. Showing through was a dark red stain, but it wasn't fresh. It had evidently started bleeding in the night but had then sealed itself again. After she secured his breakfast, she would take care of it. Now she put on her shoes and prepared to do battle for something reasonably fit to eat.

Cheyenne, Wyoming was the largest city between Omaha and Sacramento, and she could not believe that things would be no better than at Sidney. However, when the train stopped and she stood on the station platform, she understood. It was large in population only. It was far from a mature city. All she could see were temporary buildings, wooden frames covered with canvas and layers of dust. The early morning traffic was dangerous-looking, miners and cowhands wearing big boots, broad-brimmed hats, and revolvers. Not a friendly looking place, and she decided the food was probably as tough.

She pulled down her jacket, firmed up her back, and set her chin. Thus armed, she marched into the dining room. Her march halted at the door, however, for there on every wall hung rows of stuffed big-game animal heads glaring down on famished passengers. At that moment, she felt great empathy for the early Christians as they stood in the arenas of Rome and faced hungry beasts. Taking a deep breath to fortify herself, she advanced on the kitchen, but found no back-up food cooking on the stove. Everything was on the tables. Locating a place, she sat down to wait for the platters to be passed. She filled a plate with fried potatoes, over-cooked chops from an unnamed animal, and hoecakes with syrup. She had certainly failed this time. She quickly ate two soggy hoecakes and after leaving two dollars, made her way back to the train with Jordan's breakfast.

The berths had been made up and the car cleaned while she had been gone. One scarcely knew the porters were around, they were so efficient. It was as if all these services occurred as acts of magic. Jordan lay as she had left him, but now a candle tallow pallor had replaced the healthy copper tan, and his skin felt hot and dry. "Jordan?"

His eyes fluttered open and he struggled to focus on her. "I'm cold." And he began groping for more covers. She reached to the foot of the bed and spread two blankets over him.

"Here's your breakfast. Do you feel like eating it?"

"What's it look like?" The bedclothes muffled his voice.

"I'd rather not try to describe it."

"That bad, huh?"

"I'm afraid so." She made an effort to cut the chops, but they were tough as braided hemp. Now that the chops had cooled a bit, the grease congealed in white gobs around the edges and floated like little rafts in the syrup from the hoecakes. The potatoes were fried with onions and both were close to charcoal. She was glad he couldn't see the unappetizing plate, but she still had the problem of feeding him. He needed nourishment to keep up his strength, and she had no idea how she was going to provide it.

Passengers were beginning to wander back onto the car. They seemed in no hurry which was extremely unusual. Normally, people dashed from the dining room and rushed breathlessly to their seats just in time for that familiar lurch of the train that said they were moving again. Gabrielle looked up to see Melanie DeWitt making her way purposefully toward Jordan's berth.

"I noticed you left the dining room before they announced the train would be delayed here. A flash flood has damaged the track out of Laramie. We're going to wait here until it's repaired."

"Thank you for telling me. Do they have any idea how long the delay will be?" Gabrielle asked.

"The conductor didn't say, but from past experience, I'd say two or three hours. How's the patient this morning?"

"Not as well as I had hoped, Miss DeWitt. He can't eat this food, and he must have nourishment. Is there anywhere in town I could find a soft boiled egg, toast, and some tea?"

"Gabrielle, before we continue our discussion let's have an understanding. My friends call me Melanie, and I hope we're friends." She gave Gabrielle a wide innocent smile. "I have an idea. Since we have plenty of time, I'll take a stroll and see if I can come up with something more palatable that that slop they served this morning. We've had bad meals here, but this rates near the top as the worst. The cook must be new, or have a terrible hangover."

"Let me give you some money to pay for it." Gabrielle reached for her purse.

"If I can find something, it will be my contribution to Jordan's recovery. He's much too handsome to let waste away. Besides, he promised to play cards with me later this morning. He's obviously not in any condition now, and I don't want to take advantage of him. When I beat him, I want no excuses."

Gabrielle watched Melanie gather her purse and hat and hurry off the train. Then she filled the washbasin with warm water and dissolved carbolic acid crystals to make a solution. "Are you up to a change of dressing?" she asked Jordan when she returned.

"Do I have a choice?"

"No, but it would be nice if you gave your consent. After all, you owe me something for the predawn entertainment I provided."

He chortled at the remembrance. "I do at that."

"The poor man vanished this morning as soon as he was dressed and hasn't been back."

"Can't say as I blame him," Jordan said, still laughing at the memory.

At least he didn't feel warmer, she noted as she snipped the gauze away. She banked towels around his shoulder and dripped carbolic acid solution to loosen the bandage over the actual wound. He watched her intently as she worked. The gash was going to look ugly and she preferred he didn't give it his full attention. "You said you'd be back in Omaha in a couple of weeks. Do you travel this route often?" Hopefully her question would distract his thoughts from the procedure at hand.

"Lately, I have."

"Why?" She made the question sound casual and its answer unimportant.

"I have a gold mine in Idaho that I'm trying to get in operation."

"How does one go about starting up a gold mine?" She tested the bandage. It was nearly loose.

"It's not an ordinary mine. It requires a dredge."

She could feel him relax, and she noticed his eyes shift from the red-streaked gauze to the view out the window. "What is a dredge? I don't know a thing about them."

"I have a claim on the Snake River. The dredge is a flat-bottomed boat with a series of shovels on a conveyor belt. The shovels dig loads of dirt from the river bottom, bring them to the surface, and dump them into a hopper. It's washed there and the small stuff that could contain gold is saved. The big stuff is washed back into the river."

She carefully lifted the bandage. The cut looked ragged and disfiguring, but there was no sign of infection. She made a compress of the carbolic acid solution and laid it over the wound. "Have you heard of a place called Marsh Basin?'' Her attempt to keep his mind from her activities was working. He wasn't paying any attention to what she was doing. The pain must have been less, for his color was better and his eyes, clear.

''Sure. That's the stage stop before I jump off for my claim.''

Gabrielle's hands shook. ''You're getting off at Kelton, then,'' she said calmly, and hoped he didn't notice her trembling.

''Yep. Pick up my load and freight it to the river.''

So she wasn't going to be free of him, after all. Would Mr. Bailey understand her nursing this man all the way from Omaha? Would he understand the need for her to continue to change Jordan's dressings until he returned to the doctor? She would include that in her prayers though she told herself Jordan meant nothing personal to her. But so few people, unless they had had the experience, understood the relationship which developed between a nurse and patient.

She emptied and filled the basin with warm water, washed Jordan, re-bandaged the wound, wrapped him in the sheet strips, and supported his arm with the sling. ''Do you want me to shave you, or have you had your limit of attention?''

''When the beard starts to itch, I'll let you at it. My shoulder's hurting less, and I think I'd like to try a nap while we're stopped. It feels so good not to be swaying and rattling about.''

''Melanie's gone after something edible for your breakfast. May I wake you when she returns?'' She smoothed the sheet and blanket over him.

''Depends on what she finds.''

''I think she's a very resourceful lady, and I would guess you'll enjoy what she finds.''

''Then, wake me.'' He rolled over with his back to her. She tucked the covers around him and drew the bed curtain. He deserved a bit of privacy after the zoo-like gaping of yesterday.

Taking advantage of the empty car, she washed her face and re-did her hair. She kept thinking how good a bath would feel and vowed to find one, no matter how primitive, when she arrived in Marsh Basin. She even had time to read her Bible and have a few minutes of private prayer before someone knocked on the door. Melanie! Gabrielle ran to open it and there indeed stood Melanie, holding a bedtray covered with a pale yellow cloth, embroidered with soft blue cornflowers.

Gabrielle held the door while Melanie edged past. Holding up an edge of the cloth, she looked to see two boiled eggs, a covered dish which she guessed contained toast, a pot of hot water and tea. "Melanie, you are a wonder. You must tell me how you accomplished this miracle."

"I simply went to the best looking boarding house. It's run by a sea captain's widow from Boston. She was delighted to use her fine things and had a grand time fixing this tray."

Pulling back the curtain, Gabrielle watched the soundly sleeping Jordan a minute. "Seems a shame to wake him, but you've gone to so much trouble and he needs to eat." She touched his shoulder and called softly, "Jordan." He stirred and looked up at her. "Melanie is back with a lovely meal for you. Let me help you sit up."

While Gabrielle made Jordan comfortable, Melanie set the tea to steep. Then she cracked the eggs, scooped out the contents into the bowl, and seasoned them with butter and salt and pepper. She stepped in front of Gabrielle and sat both herself and the tray on the bed. It became very obvious that since she had made the successful foray, she intended to be the one to feed him.

Gabrielle returned to Melanie's seat, but she had a hard time concentrating on her reading. Melanie and Jordan laughed and visited while he ate, and they both seemed to have a wonderful time. The fact that this disturbed her, upset Gabrielle. Jordan Cooke meant nothing more to her than a patient. Then why did she feel Melanie's help was an intrusion? It certainly didn't take a nurse to feed him, she lectured herself. Any caring person could do that. But try as she would, the weight of resentment refused to leave her heart.

CHAPTER 5

IT HAD BEEN A HARD DAY and she needed the rest, but Gabrielle lay for a long time without sleeping. Many of the windows were shut or, at least, not open nearly so wide. The air hung over her, unmoving and stale. People who had not slept the first night were adapting, and the night sounds of coughing, snoring, and grinding of teeth sounded with far more intensity above the clack of the train over the rails than the night before.

It seemed highly improper to be bedded with men all around her, but it was the man below who occupied her thoughts. She pondered the twisted, tormented look on Jordan's face and the depth of feeling he had expressed when he threw away the laudanum she had tried to give him tonight. Had his earlier wounds been so severe that during their healing he had become addicted to the drug? Why else would he react with such violence and refuse the relief it brought? She had found a suitable substitute and she hoped he was sleeping soundly now. She was concerned with his exhaustion. It always amazed her how quickly and well wounds healed when the patient received adequate nourishment and plenty of rest. The nourishment she could take care of, but she couldn't force him to rest.

She looked at his reflection on the ceiling. He seemed only a bit more relaxed, for his hand lay curved into a fist. She had the feeling if anyone were to touch him at this moment, they would risk bodily harm. She had seen soldiers sleep like that, and before she learned, had narrowly missed having her face smashed by a flying fist.

She wondered if Mr. Bailey was a light sleeper. In the eight months since Ellen's death, his correspondence had told her much about himself, but the things she really wanted to know were too personal to ask, and he was certainly too much of a gentleman to mention.

She didn't remember when she went from drowsy musings to sound sleep. The shout from the berth below startled her awake, and she reacted from trained habit. Rolling from her bed, her feet barely touching the ladder, she sought the screaming, thrashing man. She threw the weight of her body across his pumping legs while attempting to restrain the flailing arm.

"Anything we can do?" she heard a heavy, deep voice outside the bed curtain ask.

Oh, land. The whole car's awake. "No, thank you. He's over-tired. Having a nightmare. Soon as I can wake him, he'll be fine." All the while, she fought to rouse him as he pitched her about like a small boat riding out a savage storm.

"Jordan, wake up." She patted his face. "Jordan!" If anything, he became more uncontrolled. She might have to call for the offered help after all. She pulled her hand back and delivered a forceful slap across his face.

His eyes, wild and blazing, flew open, and he sat

upright. "What the—," he swore. When he finally focused on her, he quieted immediately but lay, sweat pouring off him, gasping for breath. She could feel his heart racing and his hand picked nervously at the blanket. She found a towel and dried him, but it wasn't the commanding, self-assured Jordan she nursed. This was a broken, terrified, whimpering little boy.

She laid the towel aside, and curling her legs behind his back, gathered him in her arms, and held him to her as she would a frightened infant. Rocking slowly back and forth, she softly crooned an old lullaby her Negro mammy had sung years ago. Gabrielle had performed this comforting act times beyond counting during the War, but then she'd been very young and could only guess at the deep suffering inside the men.

Slowly, she felt the tension ease once more. His heartbeat slowed to a more normal pace, and the profuse sweating stopped. She felt the weight of his good arm as he placed it around her shoulders.

"Thank you," he whispered so softly that if his lips hadn't been next to her ear, she wouldn't have heard the words at all.

Pulling her legs from behind his back, she settled him down against the pillows. Light from a nearly full moon streamed across the bed, and shadowed the harsh angular planes of his face. She smiled, and unconsciously gave in to her repressed desire to smooth his hair back from his forehead. "I was afraid this might happen. You became much too tired. I'm sorry I didn't act more forcefully and demand you take an afternoon rest."

He didn't answer, but gazed at her through half-opened eyes while she softly stroked the hair from his forehead. She wondered what he was seeing, or if he was even looking at her. Perhaps his mind was miles from here, reviewing the terrors he had so recently relived. She would give a good deal to know what demons he had been fighting, for they were surely terrible, and he had not won in the many rounds he had gone with them.

Well, she would never learn that secret and since he was calm, she had best be getting back to her bed. She gathered the damp towels and spread them over the curtain rail to dry, smoothed his covers, and made a move to leave.

She felt his fingers close gently over her arm. "Please, stay a little," he whispered.

His words were thick. It suddenly occurred to her that he must be parched. "Would you like a drink of water?"

He nodded. She found her slippers and the cup, and padded to the washroom. It took three trips before his thirst was satisfied.

"Fix my pillows," he ordered, resuming his dictatorial tone. *He must be improving*, she thought wryly.

She plumped the pillows and arranged them behind his back. The night air from the partially open window blew across his bare chest, and she took his shirt from the storage compartment and draped it over him.

"Get your pillows, and I'll tuck them behind you," he said.

She stood and retrieved them from her berth. Though a bit awkward, having only one hand to work with, he helped her until she was quite comfortable.

They watched the passing desert, a seemingly endless sweep of dry sagebrush and greasewood— dreary, awful, lifeless. In the sun it would be harsh and death-ridden. The moon softened the features and cloaked them in mystical shadows, creating an enchantment that spread into the passing train.

He sought and held her hand, gently rubbing the backs of her fingers with his thumb. "Haven't had an attack of the terrors for a long time," he murmured at last, as though feeling she needed some explanation for his behavior. "Thought I had 'em licked."

"I wonder if they are ever truly silenced. Even all these years later, I hear men in the hospital suffering as you just did."

"It's a comfort to have someone realize that it's a terrible suffering." He turned his head, looked at her, and gave her a gentle smile. "Some day I want to tell you about it."

She hoped her face didn't betray the emotions running through her. What was he trying to convey to her? Someday he wanted to tell her about it. She must tell him about Mr. Bailey and the children and explain about how a patient often thinks he's in love with his nurse. She tried desperately to put her thoughts in order, so that she might make him understand.

However, while she sat struggling with these problems, he let go her hand and reaching up, cradled her face inside his large palm. He turned her to face him, bent over, and kissed her so gently and tenderly it brought tears to her eyes.

"Oh, Gabby," he whispered against her cheek. "You're the most precious thing to come into my life in years. What took you so long?"

She scarcely heard his words. Gabby! He certainly was a master at getting what he wanted from women. He took his kisses from Melanie, harsh and violent. For her, he had reserved the gentle, innocent approach. But knowing she disliked intensely being called 'Gabby,' surely he had mocked her.

She grabbed her pillows and flew up the ladder to her berth.

His hand grabbed at his shoulder. "What the . . . !" His oath cut through the quiet of the car.

She didn't care. If his shoulder hurt, it was his fault. She had done everything he would allow her to do, he had taken advantage of the situation, and now he was on his own for the rest of the night. And save for the minimum care necessary, tomorrow as well. He was no gentleman, and his actions reminded her repeatedly of that fact.

She lay in her hot, stuffy bunk, made the more uncomfortable by the burning of her face as she remembered the kiss and how much she had enjoyed it. Well, he had sneaked through her guard once, but there would not be a second time. This was their last night on the train, and she would keep a great deal of distance between them tomorrow.

Sleep only came in snatches, and morning found her nerves ragged. She knew the normal slight bags under her eyes would be enlarged into satchels. She would look a sight when she met Mr. Bailey tonight, and this knowledge made her disposition cold and biting as a December blizzard. And to add the final capping misery, her eyes burned not only from lack of sleep but from the spiraling clouds of alkali dust churned up by the passing train. A small sore caused by the alkali was forming on her lower lip, and her mouth, gritty with dust, tasted sharp and felt dry. She dreaded to think what she must look like. Dressing quickly, she looked through the curtains to see the line at the washroom was much shorter than usual at this time of morning. People were sleeping later and moving slower, so she hurried down and took her place.

When she returned, Jordan had his eyes open. "What got into you last night?" he asked, innocence filling his face and voice.

"I merely preferred my own company," she replied curtly as she stood on the ladder to pack her toilette articles into the valise. She fastened a clean collar and cuffs to her travel-weary blouse and, if one didn't examine it too closely, it looked quite presentable. She couldn't say as much for the dust-imbedded suit. She wondered if it would ever be fit to wear again.

Stepping from the ladder into the aisle, she put on a clean travel duster and reached over Jordan's head to store her valise.

"You look awful this morning," he observed. "Didn't you sleep well?"

She looked down into his bearded face. With puffy bloodshot eyes, he didn't look so fine, either. But she couldn't read any inferences. Was he asking out of concern or sarcasm? She didn't trust him to be concerned. "Your lack of tact is as boorish as your lack of manners," she snapped.

He ran his hand over his face. "I think I'm ready for a shave this morning."

She desperately wanted to tell him to shave himself. That she wanted no more to do with him. Only her sense of obligation prevented a full expression of her feelings.

The train butch interrupted her tumultuous thoughts. "Green River, Wyoming, for breakfast in ten minutes."

Her stomach rose in open rebellion at the memory of yesterday morning's unedible food in Cheyenne. "I shall shave you after breakfast."

"Not on your life. The track today is rough, winding, through tunnels, and generally not recommended for shaving along. You can shave me while we stop at Green River. There's no fine boarding house and breakfast will be a duplicate of yesterday's, only worse."

Gabrielle wished with all her heart that she didn't have to barber him. She longed to escape from him completely, but until that was possible, the less physical contact she had to have with him, the better it suited her. "Very well. I presume we will be stopped for the usual half hour, and that is ample time to accomplish the chore."

"Really hate to do it, don't you? I didn't realize I was so irresistible with a beard. Perhaps I shouldn't let you cut it off, after all."

"That would suit me perfectly," she replied, making no effort to hide her displeasure with him.

"The mood you're in, maybe I shouldn't let you near my throat."

"Do you, or do you not wish to be barbered this morning?" She stood glaring at his scraggly beard, wishing he'd say no.

"I desperately wish it. The danged thing itches ferociously," he said, and proved it by giving his face a vigorous scratching.

Rather like a dog dislodging his fleas, she thought ungraciously as she gathered his shaving things and spread them on the oil cloth. Upon testing his razor by plucking the edge with her thumb and finding it a bit dull, she sought the razor strap. "Here, hold this," she ordered.

Having shaved her father for many years, she had become very adept at the art. She stropped the razor, testing it between times, until it met with her standards.

"You go at this like a professional barber."

"What makes you think I'm not?" She allowed no levity or warmth into her voice. He'd made a fool of her for the last time.

The train push-pulled to a stop, and the hungry passengers quickly emptied the car.

Melanie came past, humming a little tune. "Good morning. You two look like you'd spent the night at a poker table—or under it." She smiled a guileless smile. "Want me to bring you back something to eat?"

"Not unless you can produce the sort of breakfast you managed yesterday," Jordan said.

"Miracles happen infrequently and Green River doesn't have the right feel. Sorry. Coffee will have to be it. Something for you, Gabrielle?"

"Coffee would be wonderful. Perhaps I'll be able to face the food at noon."

Melanie, friendly once more, and looking disgustingly rested and lovely, walked briskly down the aisle and out the door. Gabrielle felt her shoulders droop and her back sag. A long day stretched ahead and at

the end she would meet Mr. Bailey. She'd be lucky if
he let her tend his children, looking as she did. He
would most definitely give her no consideration as a
wife, especially as a replacement for the petite,
vivacious Ellen. A great sigh escaped.

"Want to tell me what that was all about?" he
asked.

"No," she answered abruptly, and proceeded to
take the basin to the washroom for water.

She replaced Jordan's face with that of her father
and, with this trick, was able to keep a steady hand
and a passive face. He couldn't talk, so the task
progressed without any further discussion.

She toweled him dry after the last rinse and let her
eyes look at his entire face for a brief moment. A
magnetism exuded from him that was nearly overwhelming. He had the dynamic charisma of a born
leader. He had to be an officer. It was a destiny he
couldn't have escaped if he'd tried. And she was as
defenseless against it as the others he had conquered.
Even Melanie, with all her experience and world-
liness, was unable to resist him.

A grin tucked itself into his cheeks. "Do you plan to
tell me what you're thinking, or are you just going to
sit and stare at me?"

Why did she let herself in for his jibes? Giving him a
piercing scowl, she quickly gathered the shaving
equipment and returned it to its case. Then, still
without speaking, she carried the water into the
washroom to be emptied. There, she took her time
drying the basin. She really should check his bandage
this morning after the strain he had placed on the
wound during his nightmare last night. However,
passengers began filing back onto the train and if the
road was as bad as Jordan had said, it was probably
better to wait until they arrived in Ogden.

The porters had removed all signs of night, and the
car returned to its daytime travel appearance. Jordan

sat slumped against the frame of the open window, a shirt knotted in his hand. He thrust it at her. "Put this on me. At least earn some of the money I'm paying you."

Anger poured through her. Earn her money! The clod! He had had the best of care and repaid her with insults and verbal abuse. She wanted to snatch the shirt and stuff it in his mouth, but by using all her self-control she managed calmly to lift it from his clenched fingers and straighten it. "This one is terribly mussed. Do you have a change?" Her voice was so noncommittal, she surprised even herself. He gave his head a flip toward the storage compartment. Inside, she found a valise which she hadn't opened previously. "Will I find it in this case?" she asked innocently.

His nearly black eyes glowered at her, and his mouth drew hard and thin. He gave the briefest of nods. She unfastened it and discovered an entire row of perfectly laundered shirts. "Which one would you like?"

Aiming a furious dagger-filled glance at her, he reached in and grabbed the first thing his hand lighted on. The shirt he chose was a magenta and grey stripe which required a buttoned-on white color. "You're sure that's the one you want?"

He nearly ground his teeth as he snarled, "Put it on!"

"Do you wish a collar, also?"

"No, I do not wish a collar." His held his voice low, but the tension running through it was deadly.

The veins stood out in his neck, and he looked ready to explode. She decided she had best get him dressed and remove herself from his sight before she angered him beyond his control. Silently she slipped his good arm into the shirt and brought it around until she could button it over the immobile arm. She took a brush from the case, and without further comment, brushed his hair as near to his liking as she could.

"There, Mr. Cooke. You are as ready for the day as I can make you," she said, a false brightness lifting her voice.

His only response was to motion for her to put down the table. She bent over, unlatched it, and placed the support leg into the hole made for it on the floor. Melanie, hands laden with a pitcher and mugs, approached as Gabrielle finished her task.

"I'm so glad you have the table ready. I couldn't hold this pitcher a minute longer." She spread three mugs and filled each with steaming fragrant coffee. "If you don't like it black, you're going to be miserable. I couldn't carry cream, and the manager bestowed a very unfriendly frown on my attempts to remove a sugar container."

"Black's fine, thank you," Gabrielle said.

Jordan grunted something unintelligible and took a sip of the hot brew. "Coffee tastes worse each time I come through. Don't think they ever wash a pot. Wait for the coffee to eat through it, then put on a new one," he complained.

"If you're in this foul a temper, you're really going to be in a snit when I clean you out today," Melanie said, producing the promised new deck of cards.

"Lady, it's only because of my kind heart and generous spirit that you're still even in the game. I didn't realize you wanted blood, but I'm definitely in the mood to oblige you." His words fairly dripping venom, he shoved the coffee pitcher and mugs to one side.

Poor Melanie, Gabrielle thought. *He's going to scalp her and post the hair in the wind.* "Are you sure you want to play with him, today? He's not feeling well and really should rest."

He raised his eyes to her face, making no attempt to hide the sparks glinting from them. "Nurse Sevier, will you be good enough to produce yesterday's stake which you selected yourself keeper of."

Gabrielle shoved her hands deep into the duster pockets. Both hands came up empty. A bolt of panic shot through her. Where was the money?

"I find your little amusement not very funny," he snarled.

"I'm not trying to be funny," Gabrielle said, casting about frantically in her memory for the whereabouts of the money. And then she remembered. She had changed dusters. The dirty one was in her valise. She reached into the storage compartment and recovered the pot, placing it carefully in the center of the table. She wanted no more to do with Jordan or the money.

She turned toward Melanie's seat. "Wait," he barked. Reaching into his pants pocket, he shoved several bills into her hand. "This is for your services. I won't be needing further attention."

She held out the money toward him. "I would like to change your bandage once more at the noon dining stop, Mr. Cooke. I fear last night you may have opened it again, causing renewed bleeding. The bandage will then grow in with the scab and be very difficult to remove."

"And I don't wish you to trouble yourself further on my account for any reason."

She felt quick-frozen from his icy stare. "As you wish," she said, suddenly empty inside and fighting the desire to cry.

CHAPTER 6

DURING THE NEXT MILES, Gabrielle scarcely heard the buzz of first-time travelers, arriving in the Utah Territory. She sat in Melanie's seat, curled into her misery. She had never been dismissed from a position in all her years and if she had been, it surely wouldn't have been accomplished in such a brutal manner. Though angry at him, the pain-drawn eyes continued to haunt her, and experience told her his wound needed tending. Doc had challenged her about her Christianity. Could she call herself Christian if she forsook her duties because of the ravings of a man half-mad with pain?

She still clutched the wad of money, uncounted, in her hand. At last, she took the bills and smoothed them. Besides five twenty dollar bills, there were two fifty dollar gold pieces. Two hundred dollars! The man was delirious! She swung her feet into the aisle and marched up to the pair.

Gabrielle stood behind Jordan, watching the muscles in his jaw twitch in pain-induced spasms, and waited for a break in the game. She hadn't long to wait. He turned his cards face up, and Melanie laid hers down.

"You still want to play?" he asked, his voice a broken croak.

"Of course," Melanie said in an off-handed manner which belied the paleness of her face. She looked up and saw Gabrielle. "Gabrielle can watch the stakes while I go freshen up." She smiled a lovely warm smile and stood in the aisle to stretch. "You won't mind for just a minute, will you?"

Yes, Gabrielle would mind. This infernal gambling is going to be the death of Jordan. And even though she didn't think that would be a terrible loss, it still went against all her instincts.

Jordan didn't look at Gabrielle, but she could feel the animosity radiating from him. Despite this, she slid into the seat opposite him, cleared her throat, and prayed for her voice to come out sounding somewhat normal. "You gave me this money in anger, and I know you didn't count it. There is far too much here. I have taken a reasonable fee. Here is the rest." She extended her hand containing four bills and the gold pieces.

He ignored the proffered hand and continued to sit, slumped against the window frame with no pillow to soften the corners. A thin coat of sweat covered the gray-colored skin of his face, and his eyes, closed to narrow slits, looked at her without focusing.

She quickly stuffed the over-paid wage into her duster pocket and scooped the poker stakes into the other pocket. He was in no condition to discuss the matter at the moment.

"You crazy man! Are you trying to kill yourself?" She flipped the table into its position against the wall and summoned a porter. "Please make up this berth." Then turning to the two men who had been assisting Jordan, she said, "Would you please help Mr. Cooke?"

Bending over him, she placed his good arm around her shoulder in an effort to assist him to his feet. "Mr. Cooke, you have to stand up. Now, help me. I can't lift you."

She felt the muscles in his body tighten into activity, and working together, they stood him on his feet. When the bed was made, he sank onto it. Gabrielle laid out her supplies, ready to attend him. She forced herself to think only of his need, not his oafish behavior. While this would be her last act of service for him, she intended do her professional best by him.

"I fired you, Gabby Sevier. Remember?" His voice was barely a whisper.

"I know, but I've never been dismissed and I don't intend to give you, of all people, that privilege. When I'm ready, I'll quit, and I'm not ready." She chose to ignore his insistence in calling her Gabby and began unwrapping the sheet strips as she talked. At least, by initiating the conversation he was making it easy for her to keep his mind off his wound.

"I called you Gabby and you didn't fly apart. What happened?"

"I can only consider the source of the insult and forgive."

"That's no insult. I like the name Gabby. What's so terrible about it?" His voice, weak and without its power, sounded no threat.

"Here's some water. Drink." She held the cup and he emptied it. "More?"

He nodded, and the porter standing by with the basin of warm water exchanged that for the empty water cup. Gabrielle poured in carbolic acid crystals and began stirring.

"That is stinkin' stuff," he commented.

"If it smelled sweet, you wouldn't trust it. Medicine always tastes or smells unpleasant." Slowly she continued to unwind the strips, praying she wouldn't find blood. However, when she came to the area of the wound, there was a fresh red stain seeping through onto the outer wrapping. Since the strips were sticking, she soaked them with the carbolic acid solution, keeping the blood stain concealed from him.

The porter returned carrying a full cup of water and a small pitcher. "Just in case the mister ain't had enough," he said.

"Thank you. You've been so helpful."

"Here." Jordan reached into his pocket and handed the porter a twenty dollar gold piece.

The startled man, struck dumb, could only stand, turning the coin over and over in his hand as though trying to assure himself it was real. Jordan waved his hand, and that motion of dismissal sent the elated porter away, but not very far. Gabrielle could see him busy, but hovering close enough so she could summon him to Jordan's bedside immediately.

"That was nice of you. He has a wife and four children and supports them on a salary of twenty dollars a month. Out of that he has to buy his uniforms and the polish he uses on the passengers' boots."

His face took on expression for the first time that morning, and he looked surprised. "How do you know that? Do you make everyone's business yours?"

She didn't want to visit with him, but she was forced to if she wanted to keep his attention from the bleeding wound. "I told you I was curious. Unfortunately, it gets me into as much trouble as it gets me out of." She saw his face relax as the anger lifted from him, and his color began returning to a more healthy tone. Now, she dripped the carbolic acid solution onto the gauze, but she had towels wrapped high enough around that he couldn't see the red blot.

"Let's get back to the subject of your name. Why the fury at Gabby?"

He surely couldn't care the tiniest bit about her displeasure at being called Gabby, other than to tease her with it. While it wasn't her favorite subject, it did keep his thoughts occupied, leaving her free to treat him. Maybe she could casually change the direction of the conversation to one less personal if she went along with it. "Persistent, aren't you? Isn't it enough to know I dislike it very much?"

"Like you, I'm curious, and I usually dig until I find the answers." His voice, the barometer of his internal strength, began to respond with its normal rich baritone timbre and, with that, his authority began to assert itself again.

How she longed to be able to lie convincingly, but her Christian principles wouldn't let her and besides, it was much too late in life to become adept at lying. She vowed, however, to tell him as little as possible.

"As a child, I asked questions until I nearly drove everyone crazy. I didn't stop with my parents. I hounded the slaves, the neighbors, guests . . . anybody who looked like a source of information. Then, instead of keeping my new-found knowledge to myself, I felt it my duty to inform anyone who would listen, and that included all the animals on the plantation. It was natural to go from Gabrielle to Gabby. Children used it to taunt me and adults to punish me. I grew to hate the name."

What was there about this man that caused her to chatter as she hadn't in years? And after she had just promised herself she would be brief in her answer. He certainly had every right to call her Gabby. She clamped her jaws tight and motioned the porter for clean water.

Out of the corner of her eye, Gabrielle watched Melanie slip quietly into her seat. She kept her head turned and stared trance-like out the window. Just how badly was Jordan beating her? Gabrielle wondered. And if she was in such deep trouble, why did she continue playing? Gabrielle praised God that in all her troubles, at least gambling had never played a part.

His face an inscrutable mask and his eyes closed, Jordan lay quietly, saying nothing. Now that she had broken the barrier, she desperately wished he would respond. He seemed unwilling or unable, however. Continuing to work on the gash, she found no sign of infection and aside from the seepage from the deepest part of the cut, the wound was doing fine. The pain that dragged at him, and his refusal to rest, were the reasons for his frightening color.

As she finished replacing the gauze, he roused. "I think you're aptly named. Gabby does fit you very well. In fact, I shall continue to call you that even in the face of your displeasure, since I don't like the name Gabrielle."

"And since you dismissed me, after I finish this dressing you won't have the opportunity to torment and insult me further." She tied the sling around his neck. "There. You are ready to do whatever you wish."

He didn't open his eyes, only nodded. She stood and drew the bed curtains. A lost lonesome feeling swept over her as she shut him away from her for the last time. Since he had occupied so much of her time for the past two days, the sense of loss was not unusual, she told herself. She was well rid of him. She would be free to concentrate on Mr. Bailey and the children. It hardly seemed possible that she would be with them this evening. Her heart began little rapid hammerings and her breath quickened at the thought.

Gabrielle turned without thinking toward Melanie's seat . . . her seat for much of the trip. Melanie sat, still lost in her world out the window. It was obvious she didn't want company, even though the seat was wide enough for the two of them.

Since there were no other empty seats in the car,

Gabrielle turned and walked into the forward Pullman car, which had some vacancies. There she could sit and make new acquaintances.

Jordan had been right about the track. It was extremely rough and even though she found people to visit with, she couldn't keep her thoughts off him. She fretted silently over his being tossed about as he tried to rest and gave an audible sigh of relief when the train slowed for the noon dining stop at Wahsatch in the Utah Territory. Even though she had promised herself she wouldn't, she couldn't stand not knowing how he had fared, and returned to his car to check on her ex-patient.

The car was empty except for Melanie who seemed not to have moved, and for Jordan behind the curtains. Gabrielle peeked in to see him sleeping soundly, a testimony to his exhaustion. Deciding he needed sleep more than food, she let him be.

It was impossible for Gabrielle to ignore anyone or anything that hurt, whether physically or mentally. It was obvious Melanie was suffering and needed a friend right now. Pausing at her seat, Gabrielle asked, "Would you like to join me in a stroll and perhaps something to eat?"

Melanie turned red-rimmed eyes on Gabrielle. "I don't think so, thanks. I'll just sit here."

Gabrielle, refusing to be put off, said, "Come on, Melanie. You'll feel better if you get some deep breaths of dust-free air." She smiled and reached out her hand to Melanie. "Please come."

Drawing a deep, unhappy sigh, Melanie gathered her purse and gloves, adjusted her hat, and reluctantly joined Gabrielle.

As they walked briskly, Gabrielle smiled at the warning in Mr. Crofutt's book, about gamblers. She hadn't counted on becoming acquainted with one and finding she liked her. Melanie was honest, making no attempt to be anything except what she was, a transcontinental gambling lady.

"I know it's against the Western Code to ask personal questions, but if it won't offend you, I would very much like to know how a lady like you became involved in such an unlikely profession." Gabrielle gulped at her presumption and suddenly wished she'd kept her question to herself.

Melanie paused and turned, looking full at Gabrielle as though pondering what was behind her interest. Apparently deciding it was only a curious and harmless inquiry, she said, "My mother died when I was six. My father was a Mississippi riverboat gambler. He had no choice but to take me with him. I grew up among the finest ladies and gentlemen, and learned gambling from the best. After my father died, I needed a change of scenery, so I became a railroad gambler."

"Don't you ever want more in your life than this? What happens when you get older?"

"If the time comes when running the rails gets boring, I'll buy my own place. I can hold cards 'til I'm ninety, and men don't care too much what a lady looks like if she can give them a good clean game. I'm good enough that I don't have to cheat. That's why Jordan and a lot of other men like to play me. They know they'll get a fair game."

Gabrielle had the feeling that that was more history about herself than Melanie had told in a lot of years. She pondered this as they slowly walked along the rails.

The call to board the train came. Gabrielle found Jordan still sleeping soundly, for which she said a prayer of thanks. He could purchase an unsavory sandwich from the butch if he became too hungry to wait for dinner in Ogden.

The trip through tunnels into Echo and Weber Canyons was spectacular. At last, there was something to see besides miles of open desert. Here, fantastic shaped rocks towered like castles in the air,

81

grand beyond description. Gabrielle found the scene at once fearful and sublime. Her heart gathered in her throat as they crossed wooden trestles over mountain rivers, churned to white water by the boulders they beat against.

Shortly after entering the narrows of Weber Canyon, Melanie pointed out a single green pine growing in a desolation of rock and sage. "That's called the 'thousand mile pine.' It marks the distance we've come from Omaha. Also means we're not far from Ogden and you need to wake Sleeping Beauty. I hope he's rested. I want another go at him," Melanie said.

"I'll wake him, but haven't you had enough punishment at his hand?"

"I've had too much, and I mean to recoup my losses before he squirms out of my clutches at Kelton. No one's luck can go this long without a change. And believe me, he's due for a fall."

Sticking her head through the curtains, Gabrielle found Jordan, in spite of the rough ride, still sleeping deeply. She really disliked waking him, but since they were changing to the Central Pacific line which meant moving the baggage and all their belongings to a different car, she had no choice.

"Mr. Cooke, I am informed we are nearing Ogden. It is necessary that you awaken."

He rolled over and looked at her. "Gabby, did you ever try saying things in a less formal manner?" He yawned and stretched his good arm. "That was the best sleep I've had in months."

His color was what she presumed to be normal for him, and he looked truly rested. Hopefully the wound would cease hurting so intensely and he would stop pushing himself so hard until it had time to heal a bit more. "You're welcome, and now I would like to clear up the matter of the overpayment of my wages."

She took the money from her pocket and handed it to him. He captured her hand and folded it around the bills and coins. "I want you to have it, all of it. I don't need it and somehow I feel you do. You've spent your entire trip waiting on a surly, ill-tempered man, enduring his insults like a lady, and not complaining. Please let me salve my conscience the only way I know."

Gabrielle heard very little of what he said, for the warmth and strength from his hand traveled rapidly through her, and she found herself reluctant to break away from his hold.

"Gabby, please take the money."

He apparently intended to hold her hand around it until she agreed. All right, she would take it, she decided. He was right. She did need the money. She had put up with more from him than anyone she had nursed in recent memory. She had endured a great deal to earn the money, and he had paid well for her services. They were even.

CHAPTER 7

THE PORTER CAME and put away the bed and Gabrielle now sat opposite Jordan. She would have preferred to exchange places with Melanie, but didn't feel comfortable suggesting it, since it was obvious Melanie wished solitude for now. Also, Jordan was alert enough to make some other jabbing comment about her name. She had no idea what it would be, but he would do it just the same, and in a voice guaranteed to carry throughout the car. Gabrielle could see no graceful way to escape occupying her assigned seat.

"Trying to think of a way to get out of sitting with me?" he asked suddenly.

Startled by his uncanny ability to read her mind, she stammered, and her flustered attempt to answer him gave her away. The creases deepened around his mouth and eyes, signifying his delight at her discomfort.

Making a considerable effort to regain her composure, she chose to ignore his question. "Would you like to change your shirt before arriving in Ogden?"

"What's wrong with this one?" He tugged at it with his fingertips.

Why did she find it impossible to mind her own business? Even if he did look comical, it was no concern of hers. She had chosen this topic, though, and he would demand that it be discussed until he was satisfied.

"It makes you look like a barker at a side show, but then perhaps that's the image you wish to portray." She kept her voice calm and impersonal. He was not going to rile her again. They only had a few more hours together, and she was determined to remain unruffled no matter what he said.

"You sound like a mother, or worse, a wife. I intend to wear this choice for the remainder of the day even in the face of your disapproval." He settled himself deeper into his seat as though preparing to meet her anticipated attempt to strip the shirt from his back.

She wanted to laugh. It was the same symbolic act of defiance as when a small child plants his feet, folds his arms, and sets his little jaw. *Well, Mr. Jordan Cooke, you can look a clown the rest of the year for all I care!*

"As you wish." She concluded the conversation by letting him have his way. This would assure a respite from his boorish behavior, she hoped.

Picking up her guidebook, she read snatches of the advice and information concerning the Utah Territory. Between paragraphs she admired the canyon carved by the Weber River that changed from high narrow walls to lovely green valleys as it wound along beside the train tracks. She attempted to ignore him completely. Not an easy thing to accomplish when he insisted on sprawling his feet and legs across much of the available compact floor space and jiggling his foot in an unceasing nervous dance.

Her obvious lack of response to anything he did apparently deflated him, and his defiance began to shrink. At last he said, "What's the book say about Ogden? I've never bothered to buy a copy."

She silently handed over the book, and gazed intently out the window. She could feel his eyes on her, however, staring with rude insolence. *Oh, Lord. Please don't let me blush. He'll laugh at me again, for sure.* The thought of his laughter at her expense was enough to make her angry, and the unwanted blush materialized, much to her annoyance.

Under the tension the minutes crept by, but finally he tired of the game and actually began reading her book. She deliberately forced her ramrod posture to relax and so allowed a slight droop in her rigidly held shoulders and back. Her long legs were beginning to cramp at being squeezed too tightly together and curled back under the sofa-type seat in an effort to evade any contact with Jordan. She uncrossed her ankles and gingerly slid a foot forward into a small space next to the wall. He immediately reshuffled his sitting position and allowed an errant leg to pin the calf of her leg against the wall.

"Mr. Cooke! Kindly move your leg and permit me a small space for my extremities. I do not care on which end of the seat you choose to sit, but when you have made your decision, then please manage somehow to occupy only your space."

A smile not unlike that of the Cheshire cat spread across his face. "If you will notice carefully, you will see that I am sitting across the entire seat. I, therefore, would find it impossible to place my extremities at one end or the other."

He did have the decency to speak softly, but she was vibrantly aware that the rich golden timbre that marked his voice so distinctively, had returned. He was definitely on the mend and could well do without her ministrations. However, she had no intention of letting him drive her from her place. That would be admitting defeat in their small battle, and she wasn't beaten yet.

"I am aware that you are lounging across the entire

seat. Were you to sit in a proper manner, there would be ample room for both of us to comfortably place our feet on the floor."

"And if I don't?"

The arrogant creature sprawled in open defiance and moved his feet to take over more of the available space. What would she do? She felt toyed with; he, the amused cat, and she, the cornered mouse. Suddenly, with no more than a split-second's thought, she kicked the shin nearest her with the all the force she could muster in so small a space.

"Ow!" he wailed.

"Move!" she demanded between clenched teeth.

He lifted the injured leg and rubbed the offended spot, all the while glaring into her face. She moved her other leg into the relinquished space, and settled herself to take permanent possession. *One small victory for the South*, she thought triumphantly, and returned her gaze to the passing scenery.

The tracks followed closely along the Weber River. After so many hundred miles of seeing nothing but sagebrush and dirt held firm in places by occasional clumps of grass, it was a special treat to watch water boil and roll its way down the canyon and out into the wide valley of the Great Salt Lake below. The train seemed to spurt from the mouth of the canyon and dip quickly down onto the flood plain of the river, now flowing calm and wider along willow-lined banks. They entered Ogden from the south, and from her side of the car, Gabrielle watched a giant lake spreading to the west as far as the eye could see. She longed to be able to get close enough to explore the salt-saturated water she had heard such tales about, but a considerable number of miles lay between Ogden and the lakeshore. Her chances looked very slim.

At this time, the conductor came rolling through the car, his walk not unlike the gait of a riverboat captain. "Mr. Cooke, are you well enough or will you require special assistance in leaving the train?"

He's just fine, Gabrielle thought, but since she hadn't been addressed, she sat quietly.

"I do believe I could use some help," Jordan replied. "I also seem to have acquired an injury to my leg." His eyes pierced her as he spoke.

Oh dear. Maybe she had kicked him harder than she planned. She almost reached down to lift his pants leg and survey the damage, then thought better of it. He had paid her and dismissed her. She was now nothing but a lady sharing this space with him. She folded her hands properly in her lap and returned her gaze to the window and the passing view.

"I thought perhaps you would need attending, so I had our telegrapher wire ahead for a wheelchair to be placed at your disposal."

"Thank you. I appreciate your thinking of my welfare." He accented the word *your*, and Gabrielle felt the knife penetrate.

"Nurse Sevier?"

The conductor was speaking to her. But, of course . . . he knew nothing of her being discharged and would naturally assume she was still Jordan's dutiful nurse. She turned from the window and smiled a rather stiff smile.

"We'll provide you help in assisting Mr. Cooke from the train, and the wheelchair will be waiting at the foot of the steps."

The conductor actually bowed, and she had the terrible urge to produce a scepter and strike him on both shoulders, dubbing him a knight. The tension and sleeplessness of the trip must be causing her to hallucinate. Struggling for normalcy, she found her calm nursing voice, and without looking at Jordan, said to the conductor, "You have been so helpful. Mr. Cooke and I appreciate your thoughtfulness in anticipating his needs." She gave him what she hoped was a recognizable imitation of the dazzling smile Melanie so easily bestowed in similar circumstances. Apparently it was effective, for the dear man blushed furiously and removed his hat to mop his brow.

Gabrielle, in her unschooled naïveté, found she enjoyed the results. Whatever possessed her to do a thing like that? she scolded. Her behavior was becoming unrecognizable. In five short days since leaving Nashville, she had changed dramatically—for the worse. She most surely was in need of some serious prayer for forgiveness when she could secure a few private moments.

Amid the usual clanking of metal as the cars jammed against their hitches, the hissing steam from the brakes, and the high-pitched squealing of the wheels as they locked and slid on the tracks, the train lurched to its final stop on the long trip. Now began the interminable wait while the exchange of mail, luggage, and personal belongings was made from one railroad company to the other.

Why this should take so long, she couldn't see, since the tracks of the Central Pacific ran parallel to the Union Pacific here at the station. People began pouring from the cars and soon the roofed-over platform was teaming with activity. Gabrielle watched as a wheelchair, maneuvered through the crowd by a porter, was deposited as promised at the foot of the steps.

She began gathering her things to leave with the rest of the passengers. She did not wish to inflict herself on Jordan any longer than necessary.

"Where do you think you're going?" His voice bore through the car like a cannon.

Why did he seem to feel he still commanded her attention and care? He had made it abundantly clear he wished to be rid of her.

"I plan to remove my possessions and myself from this train car. It is my understanding that we have arrived at the point where it is necessary." She continued to search the storage compartment behind his head.

"I don't find your pawing through that cubbyhole like a pack rat particularly enjoyable. Do you mind waiting until I move?"

"I do mind. I have no idea how long it will be until your servants arrive to attend your passage to the wheelchair. It is not my intention to sit and entertain you until their arrival."

With her few effects now in order, she turned to step into the aisle. The way was blocked by Melanie, valise in hand. "Are you in need of some help in getting Jordan off the train?" she offered.

"I am no longer responsible for anything Mr. Cooke wants or needs. He has made other arrangements. But," she added, "he would undoubtedly enjoy your company." Why did Gabrielle have this terrible urge to cry? And what was this sinking, empty feeling doing in the pit of her stomach? She must make her escape before she let some uncontrolled emotional outburst embarrass them all.

She started to push past Melanie, but was brought up short as Jordan snaked out his hand and gripped her arm. "Nurse Sevier, you have been paid, and paid very well I might add, to care for me until such time as our paths cease to cross. I had no idea you were the type to accept money and leave without fulfilling your promised obligations."

She whirled and glared down at him. "You very clearly told me this morning that my services were no longer necessary."

"And you told me you had never been dismissed and you wouldn't stand for it. I haven't heard a word about your decision to quit. Have I missed something?"

He hadn't missed anything. She had failed to mention to him when she planned to discontinue her services. However, he wasn't going to get an apology. "I made the decision that my last act of service would be the changing of your bandage. What happened to your mind reading ability?"

"It fails me occasionally and this is one of those times. I expect that you shall attend me until our ways part of necessity." His grip loosened, and he removed his hand from her arm. His features softened and his voice took on a low, intimate tone. "Or until you tell me you have quit my service."

The inside of her mouth turned sand-dry, and she longed to lick her suddenly parched lips. Not trusting herself to speak, she tipped her head in a slight acknowledging nod, and found herself slowly being willed to look into his eyes, green gold-flecked pools of velvet gentleness.

Drawn into a silky web, Gabrielle became entwined with Jordan for a single enchanted moment. The magic spilled into timelessness along thin shimmering strands and sounded faint silvery bell-tones.

"I repeat," Melanie said. "May I be of any help?"

Her words ripped the fragile bonds. Gabrielle fought returning back from timeless space where only the two of them existed, felt violated at the destruction, and had no understanding of why. As their eyes cleaved one final transitory twinkling longer in an attempt to recapture the moment, she knew that Jordan, too, felt a special devastation.

Unable to trust her voice, Gabrielle nodded at Melanie. She then returned her valise to the seat and with trembling hands, searched the storage compartment for his things.

"Sit down, Mel, while Gabby gets things packed."

His voice, full of its usual imperious commanding overtones, gave not the slightest hint of any intrusive emotion, while she still couldn't speak, at least, not in a normal voice. *Oh, Gabrielle. You've probably imagined the whole incident.* This thought left her empty and cold inside, and she began doubting the wisdom of ever leaving Nashville at all.

The Pullman Palace car was unoccupied save for the three of them when the two porters entered, obviously there to assist Jordan from the train. "The mister ready to leave?" one of them asked.

"Mel, you carry the valise and Gabby, take good care of that portfolio," he instructed before allowing the two men to help him to his feet.

After limping up the aisle of the car in a most pathetic manner and causing the porters to nearly carry him down the steps, Jordan was finally seated in the chair. One of the porters relieved Melanie of the burden of the valise and started to take the portfolio Gabrielle carried.

"Hang on to that for me, Gabby. Got some important papers in it."

He didn't look directly at her as he spoke and this was unusual. Ordinarily he watched her face intently as though he could read every thought registered there. Perhaps he didn't want her to see the spark in his eye that would tell her he had played a wonderful joke on her a few minutes ago and was now free to enjoy it immensely.

"Let's go to the Ogden Junction Hotel," he suggested. "We can set our bags in the lobby and relax in their overstuffed chairs. I don't relish spending the next hours in that old barn they call a depot, crammed on a wooden bench."

"The hotel management doesn't appreciate people using the lobby as a waiting room or haven't you discovered that fact?" Melanie questioned.

"If you slip the desk clerk a little something, he doesn't seem to see you at all. I'm surprised you haven't discovered *that* fact," he said.

Melanie, disregarding his remarks, walked beside the wheelchair as the second porter pushed it along the wide plank walk to the hotel. She and Jordan bantered amiably as they moved along, ignoring Gabrielle.

The crush of people closed immediately behind the passage of the wheelchair, and she had to force her

92

way through the crowd of blue-coated, brass-buttoned officers and solders; Levi-clad miners and prospectors; longhaired, buckskin-dressed mountaineers and trappers; red-blanketed Indians from Indian country to the north, west, and south; and Chinamen still wearing the primitive pointed-top bamboo hat. Mixed with the well-to-do, well-dressed, aristocratic travelers from the eastern cities, it made an intriguing panorama, which occupied her thoughts. She could conveniently postpone pondering the unfamiliar sensations so recently experienced. Maybe, if she kept very busy, she could avoid ever having to face them at all.

Jordan's small entourage arrived in the hotel lobby where he paid the clerk to be understanding and blind. Jordan also tipped the porters extravagantly after they fussed over and attended to his slightest whim. The longer she watched, the more certain she became that he had only tricked her into thinking something special had passed between them. She could thank him for one thing, however. Now she knew the feelings she wanted between her and Mr. Bailey. Only she wanted no interruption so that she might linger a very long time with him in that wonderful space.

At last Jordan seemed happy with the arrangements for his comfort and the porters left. Gabrielle leaned the portfolio against his chair. Since she had plenty of time, she planned to investigate checking her valise with the rest of her luggage.

"I'm going to see if I can find a small table," Melanie said. "I intend to win back the money you've pocketed—and more."

"Mel, do you really think that's wise? I'm still on a lucky streak and if you insist on playing, I'm going to clean you out."

Gabrielle couldn't believe her ears. He seemed to be pleading with Melanie not to play. It had to be because he was tired. It certainly wasn't because he cared whether or not he bankrupted Melanie. He did a great job of acting over his leg. What was to prevent him from using the same tactics to put an end to the poker game. Maybe he feared Melanie would win back her losses. Whatever the outcome, Gabrielle was determined not to stay around to witness it.

"I think I shall locate the Central Pacific depot and see about checking my valise for the remainder of the trip," she said, feeling she had best advise him of her plans since she did not wish to cause a scene by terminating her service to him. There was so little time left now until she was in Kelton, it wasn't worth the embarrassment.

"Take mine and check it to Kelton, too," he ordered. While he addressed Gabrielle, his eyes never left Melanie. "You coming back to watch the slaughter?"

"No, I think not. I prefer to do some sightseeing."

"Not much to see here," he observed, watching Melanie break open a new deck of cards. "Why don't you take the Utah Central down to Salt Lake City? Costs less than three dollars, and I know you have the money. Do your sightseeing and some shopping. They have fine stores there. Lots of the first-timers will be going. Our train west won't leave until about seven tonight."

His mood swings were nearly impossible to understand. He was acting like he really cared that she pass the waiting time by enjoying herself. There was the clue . . . acting, she decided. He ran from real feelings like an antelope, and seemed to successfully stay ahead of anything meaningful. *What did he fear?* Since he allowed only the briefest of cracks in his facade, and their time together was nearly over, she knew she would never know the answers.

Leaving the hotel and locating the ticket office, she checked the two small bags. She found her way to the Utah Central and happily bought a round-trip ticket.

Many of the people she had met from the other Pullman car were also making the side excursion and so she settled into her seat, anticipating the afternoon of adventure.

Instead, however, she found she felt like an outsider. Her devotion to Jordan had kept her separate when their friendships were being established. While everyone treated her with respect and courtesy, none invited her to join them. So she set her jaw and determined she would have an enjoyable time, with or without a companion.

The train passed the point of a rather high hill and she could see Salt Lake City. It was built on the lower slopes of a large fan of earth washed down from the Wasatch mountains toward the shores of the Great Salt Lake. Gabrielle watched in awe the steep rise of the snow-capped Wasatch range behind the city, deepening to the east in layer after indistinct layer of rugged mountains. As she strolled east from the depot, she found the city clean, orderly, beautifully planned and planted, and prosperous.

She made her way past the large square of ground devoted to Church buildings, including the Mormon tabernacle which she had read about in her guidebook. The place was a beehive of activity centered about a partially-constructed building framed with scaffolding. It was being built of huge granite cubes. This must be the new temple she had read about. She was most cross with Jordan at the moment for he had failed to return her guide book, and she couldn't remember more about it.

Jordan's appraisal of the stores was accurate. She found the church-owned Zion Co-operative Mercantile Institute to be a very progressive store and with her newly acquired wealth, she browsed happily looking for something to take to Sarah and Amy, and perhaps even an appropriate book for Mr. Bailey. At last she settled on a book of essays and small handmade dolls for the girls.

The time flew by and she hastened to the station, fretting all the way that she had overstayed and would miss the train back to Ogden. Her worries were well-founded, for the conductor stood with his hand raised as she came hurrying from the station. He assisted her up the steps and gave the signal. She wasn't even seated when the train gave its now-familiar tug-lurch and with her hands full of bundles, she nearly pitched headlong down the aisle. A strong hand steadied her and then the kindly gentleman offered her a seat next to his wife.

All during her short excursion, Gabrielle couldn't remember when she had felt so carefree. She had a nearly uncontrollable urge to giggle out loud, because the happiness kept bubbling to the surface and demanding to be expressed.

As the train entered the Ogden station, she reorganized her packages so that she had a free hand to extend to the porter assisting her down the steps. Leaving the train, her feet flew along the boardwalk, and she hummed a breathless little tune as she made her way back to the hotel.

Gabrielle entered the lobby, and stopped short. So many people filled the room it was impossible to do more than squeeze inside. She attempted to inch along the wall toward where she had left Jordan and Melanie, but a large Boston fern blocked her path. Now she stood trapped and unable to see much around her.

The room grew strangely quiet, and Gabrielle noticed that the men, all facing the same way, were peering intently across the lobby, their fists clenching wads of money. Although she could only see people's backs, tension fairly cracked in the silence, and she knew she had arrived at a crucial moment.

Jordan spoke in a conversational tone, but in the hush, she could hear him easily. "I'll see your five hundred and raise you a thousand."

"Cripes," a man in front of her said. "That pot's got to be over four thousand dollars."

"Yep," another answered, "and I'm bettin' on him."

So that's why so many men were holding money. They were betting on the bettors. The Bible was right. Sin, once permitted entrance, did increase in a frightening manner. She suddenly felt unclean, inside and out, and yet she could see no way out of there, except to elbow her way through.

"I'll meet your thousand and call," Melanie's cool voice rang into the stillness.

It was so hushed, Gabrielle could hear people breathing. The crowd seemed to lean forward even further, straining in the effort to see the cards. Of course, this was impossible, and the majority had to rely on those standing around the table to pass the word.

"Your luck's run down, Mel. Two aces beat two kings."

The room went wild. The groans of the losers were drowned in the cheers of those who had bet on Jordan. Gabrielle made use of the movement to slip through the crowd until she stood beside Jordan's chair. Incredibly, he and Melanie were sitting nearly as she had left them hours ago, but instead of looking fresh and vibrant, they both appeared drained. Jordan's face, while not grayish and clammy as when she had forced an end to their extended playing on the train, still held lines drawn thin around his eyes and mouth. The slender white scar down the side of his face stood out, giving him a dangerous look she had never noticed.

His eyes, slitted and impossible to read, turned on her as he became aware of her presence. "Did you have a good trip?" His thumb riffled the cards as he talked to her.

"I had a lovely time, thank you."

"Did a little shopping, I see."

"Yes. The stores were a delightful surprise, and so was the city."

"Stop and talk to anyone?" That familiar crooked grin told her what he meant.

"Would you believe me if I told you no?" She couldn't contain a full-blown smile.

"Not for a minute, Gabby, my love. Not for a minute." And his grin broke into a thin smile. He moved from his slumped position in the green brocade upholstered wingback and sat up.

"If you'll give me back your cards, I'll deal a new game," Melanie said.

Gabrielle looked at her for the first time. The tension was finally taking its toll of her freshness, too. The rouge on her cheeks stood out in harsh contrast to the pale skin underneath. Gabrielle wanted to interrupt the game, get them both out in the fresh air. However, they were adults, and she determined she had issued her last ultimatum regarding either of them. They could sit here and play until they missed their train. She felt no further responsibility.

The air hung blue with the smoke of cigars and pipes. She could taste the tobacco on her lips, and her eyes began to burn because of it. She was grateful to all those men who chewed. Although the spittoons were messy, they at least didn't contaminate her breathing air.

"You two going to play another hand?" a coarse voice bawled from the center of the teaming crowd.

"I think not," Jordan answered, and moved to stand.

Melanie went into her familiar pout. "If you don't play, how am I going to win back my money?" She tipped her head in a coy, teasing fashion. While her tone was light, the look in her eyes hinted at desperation.

"You can't. Honestly, Mel, you've never been so

98

addicted to losing your shirt before. Let's take a break. We can play on the train, later." Jordan threw his cards on the table and rose stiffly to his feet.

The men cleared the room slowly, wandering out in search of more entertainment. Jordan reached down and picked up the portfolio.

Straightening, he shot a glance at the grandfather clock standing next to the registration desk. "Is it that late? I'd hoped we'd have time to go into Ogden for a good dinner. Won't be able to now. Train should be ready to leave in a half hour."

He started to walk away and Gabrielle fell into step beside him. As though having forgotten Melanie, and suddenly remembering, he paused and turned. "Coming, Mel?"

"I don't think so. I'm not especially hungry, and that food is only edible if one is on the verge of starvation."

"You have described my condition perfectly so I should enjoy a great meal. See you on the train."

Gabrielle felt guilty about leaving Melanie, and she looked over her shoulder as Jordan hurried her across the lobby. Probably feeling that she was unobserved, Gabrielle saw that Melanie allowed her body to slump, and cradled her forehead in her hands, raised high by elbows resting on the table in front of her. She seemed to shrink and wilt into a tiny shapeless bundle of despair and defeat. *Why does she insist on playing?*

Gabrielle, pierced by the pitiful sight of the solitary figure and remembering that she had no family, longed to rush back and comfort her. That would be futile, however, for Melanie would never admit her desperate circumstances. And so Gabrielle accompanied Jordan out into the welcome fresh air and stood with him to admire the orange-gold sun sink into the Great Salt Lake.

CHAPTER 8

DINNER AT THE LONG tables in the Union Pacific depot added to the string of ill-prepared meals Gabrielle had endured. How she longed for some good ingredients and her own stove. While not a great cook, she certainly could prepare a better meal than anything she had tasted to date. She most definitely could not do worse.

The harsh noises of clattering cookware and banging table service echoed and reverberated through the barren two-story building. This, in accompaniment with the bawdy, raucous talk of men too long in the mountains, increased Gabrielle's distaste for the lumpy paste attempting to pass for mashed potatoes and drowned in thick, clotted gravy over-seasoned with grease and pepper.

Her stomach revolted at the sight and odor, and her head took up the mutiny, pounding its defiance in sharp measured beats. She dabbled her fork in the contents of her plate while marveling at the dispatch with which Jordan packed away his food. Not being able to use knife and fork in tandem, he picked up the seared meat in his fingers and tore at it in a most unmannerly fashion. From the struggle he was having, though, she didn't think the steak possible to cut with less than a meat cleaver, and so she forgave him his savage behavior.

When Jordan asked for a second helping, she could no longer endure the stale cooking and tobacco odors mixed with the essence of unwashed bodies. "Please excuse me. I feel in need of some air before we board the train."

"Sure. If you get on before I do, save me a seat." He licked his fingers in preparation for the next round of steak.

"I can't guarantee that will be possible. I shall try." *But not very hard.* She was tired, and the anticipation of meeting her new family stretched her nerves into taut strings of tension. The throbbing headache bore testimony to this, and she didn't feel up to sparring with Jordan. What she desperately wanted was a quiet corner where she could shut her eyes and relax, uninterrupted.

After a brisk airing along the plank walkway, she sought her second-class railroad car. The final miles had to be spent in these accomodations, since she was now a day passenger making a local stop.

While the seats were upholstered, they were far less comfortable than those in the Pullman car. The designers must have all been short people, she decided. There was little room for her legs and when her companion occupied the seat facing her, there would be even less. Especially if it happened to be Jordan.

She opened the window and felt a spring breeze lift the stale air. Small oil lamps along the walls hadn't been lit yet, and early evening shadowed the car. She rested her head against the window frame and closed her eyes. The cool air fanned her flushed face and gradually dispelled her headache. She was feeling much better by the time she heard Jordan's voice precede him to where she sat.

"Thanks for keeping me a spot," he said, and folded his huge frame into the inadequate space.

Because she didn't want a repeat of the scene earlier in the day, she said, "So that we might complete this trip in some semblance of comfort, shall we agree now on the division of the available space for our feet?"

He laughed. "Might be a good idea. I would prefer my other leg remain whole." He settled himself with his back against the window frame and his legs stretched partially into the aisle. "That give you enough room?"

Actually, it gave her most of the room if she sat near the aisle and extended her legs toward the window. "I am as comfortable as one can expect in these poorly designed seats, but your legs aren't going to remain unscathed if you leave them in the aisle."

"I don't think the car's going to be too crowded tonight. Lots more people seem to travel over the weekends." He rested his head against the window frame as she had done hers and shut his eyes. Soon, judging by the even rise and fall of his chest, he appeared to be sleeping soundly.

Members of the rough crowd in the dining room began clomping down the aisle, taking care, however, to step over Jordan's feet. Their talk seemed subdued in deference to his sleeping. Jordan seemed capable of controlling people's lives, even in his sleep.

Despite his prediction that there would be a limited number of travelers tonight, the car was nearly full when the first lurch rattled through the train, and it began its slow departure from Ogden.

A small flash of alarm jarred Gabrielle. Where was Melanie? Then she remembered. Melanie, traveling to San Francisco, would naturally be comfortably aboard one of the Silver Palace sleeping cars. These were the Central Pacific's answer to the Pullman, Collis Huntington and his partners having refused to allow George Pullman to place his cars on their tracks.

Gabrielle yearned to peek inside them, but she, now demoted to second-class, was no longer permitted the run of the entire train. If they were to see Melanie again, she would have to come to them.

Storage facilities were limited to a small cylinder-shaped container mounted on the wall near the ceiling, and so Gabrielle kept her gifts with her on the seat. The brakeman lit the lamps, and the flickering flames cast soft ever changing shadows over the battered interior of the car and its passengers. There was enough light, though, for Gabrielle to enjoy looking at the dolls she had purchased once again.

She carefully untied the string and unfolded the crackling tan wrapping paper quietly as she could so as not to disturb Jordan. There, exposed and cradled in her lap, lay Sarah's doll. Ellen had described Sarah as a miniature Gabrielle, both in looks and actions. That meant she had nondescript features, pale skin, and was too thin and tall for her age. *Poor Sarah*, Gabrielle sighed. Because Sarah was plain, Gabrielle had chosen a frilly, elegant doll. She fingered the soft coral silk of the gathered skirt and the delicate-patterned lace edging around the bonnet. This was a show doll to place on Sarah's bed. It's hand-painted porcelain face was so life-like, it would be easy to talk to when everyone else was tired of listening.

Gabrielle had always wanted a doll like this, but she was such a little mother she had been given baby dolls or stuffed rag dolls—dolls she could nurse and tend. If Sarah at six was a miniature Gabrielle, she would treasure her fancy doll above all the others.

Jordan squinted an eye open and said in a matter-of-fact voice, "Not a very practical choice for a little ranch girl. Sure you didn't buy it for yourself?"

That was exactly what she had done, but it vexed her that he should guess. She forced her voice to match his. "I realize it is not for everyday playing. Knowing my sister, I'm sure both girls have numerous dolls for that. Every little girl, though, longs for a special doll. Especially if the child is not beautiful herself."

"Who's this one for?"

"Sarah. She's six and since Ellen's death has taken over the mothering of three-year-old Amy. At least, that is what Mr. Bailey writes."

"You going to marry Bailey?"

His abrupt question startled her. "That matter has not been discussed." How she wished Jordan would go back to sleep and stop inquiring into her future. He was forcing her to face facts she longed to postpone dealing with.

Gabrielle watched Jordan's eyes look up past the doll. She followed his lead to observe Melanie standing in the aisle. "What a cozy arrangement you two have. Glad to see you've drawn a truce over leg room." She looked amazingly renewed with her make-up and hair repaired, and clean collar and cuffs refurbishing the travel-tired blouse.

Gabrielle became aware of her own appearance. She must freshen her toilette. How would she ever explain her untidiness to Mr. Bailey? Hastily rewrapping the doll, she excused herself. "I'm leaving for a bit if you'd like to sit here and visit."

"I hadn't planned on visiting. I have only a short time in which to get even with Jordan for this afternoon. I don't want him leaving me at Kelton, a man rich on my money."

"Mel, you're not going to win." Jordan pronounced those words as one would a benediction, definite and final.

"Oh, but I am," she said with a beguiling smile, and produced a deck of cards.

"Mel, this is your last warning. I am going to clean you out, down to your last dime, if you persist in this. I hold most of your money, but you still have some pocket change and enough to stake a game with somebody else. Quit while you can."

Jordan's face had grown hard. Gabrielle couldn't understand how Melanie would dare play with him after his warning, reinforced by his altered expression. It seemed impossible that this was the same man she had been discussing dolls with a few minutes earlier.

Gabrielle turned and walked quickly to the front of the car and the washroom, the sound of shuffling cards following her down the aisle.

As she recombed her hair and washed her face, Gabrielle felt an urgent need to talk with the Lord. Her life, until she boarded the train in Nashville, had been a predictable set of habits. The interruption of her routine had set her off balance. She didn't seem able to find time to read her Bible, a thing she did regularly each morning and evening. And she had talked often with God as she would a dear friend. Perhaps it was the complete lack of privacy. She had never spent so many days continually surrounded by people, with no place to retreat for a few moments.

Dear Lord, I don't mean to presume to tell You what to do. And I know and have had much proof the past days that gambling is a terrible sin, but it would surely be nice if Melanie could win a bit today. If Your intent, though, is to turn her from a life of gambling, I will surely praise You and understand the reason for her predicament.

Gabrielle, trying to regroup her thoughts, opened her eyes and looked down at her suit. It was impregnated with alkali dust, fine as face powder. She doubted she would ever totally rid her traveling clothes of it. The decision to leave her duster and whisk broom in the valise, now out of reach in the baggage car, was not a wise one.

With both hands she clutched the washstand and felt the nervous tremors run through her body at the thought of meeting Mr. Bailey. *And Lord, stay close by my side when we reach Kelton. I have no idea what to say to Mr. Bailey and I'm frightened. Frightened I'll say the wrong thing, or too much of the right thing. You know my weakness, Lord. Help me. Amen.*

She felt better following the prayer and, hopefully, after brushing off what dust she could, using her hand, she looked a bit more tidy. With her thoughts still leaping ahead to the first meeting with Mr. Bailey, she stepped into the aisle to return to her seat. However, a tight knot of passengers had collected in that general area. A hush had fallen over the car and Gabrielle again experienced the tension she had felt earlier that day in the hotel lobby.

"I'll see your hundred and raise you five hundred." Jordan's voice, while not loud, was easily heard in the anticipatory silence filling the car.

There was a pause, then Melanie said, "Excuse me."

The crowd parted and Melanie swept through. Gabrielle stepped out of the aisle into a vacated seat area to allow Melanie clear passage to the convenience. Her eyes, glazed over and unseeing, bore past Gabrielle with no recognition. Gabrielle, concerned that Melanie might be ill, followed her, pulled aside the curtain that provided minimum privacy, and watched Melanie pull some money from her stocking.

"Melanie, is that all the money you have?" Gabrielle asked softly.

However, Melanie failed to focus on Gabrielle. She dropped her skirts and hastened back up the aisle. The crowd made way for her to return to her seat.

Gabrielle could see nothing of the action and had to depend on what she heard. Nothing was being said and the silence was awful.

"Can't you cover the bet?" Jordan finally asked.

"Will anyone loan me the money? I'm good for it," Melanie begged.

"Sister, I've followed your luck all day," a well-dressed gentleman spoke up, obviously from the first-class section. "You've scarcely won a hand from this fellow. I think you're too much of a risk."

"But I do have a winning hand. I'll show you."

"You won't show anyone," Jordan said, his voice a low, ugly snarl.

Again, only silence. Gabrielle felt her fingernails biting into the palms of her hands.

"In that case, the stakes are mine," she could hear Jordan distinctly.

"Let's see the hands," someone demanded.

"Yes," chimed in another. "We'd all like to know how it would have come out if she'd been able to come up with the money."

A murmur rippled through the crowd. "A four and seven! Shoulda loaned the lady some money," someone close to the action bellowed.

Gabrielle watched the crowd return to their seats. Melanie, her eyes wide in her stress-pinched face, gathered her things into trembling hands. Without another word, she returned to her sleeping car.

Jordan had already leaned back against the wall and closed his eyes by the time Gabrielle was able to return to her seat. He gave no sign that he noticed her and this left her free to think her own thoughts.

The Lord certainly had brought Melanie to her knees, Gabrielle decided. Now, since Gabrielle seemed to be the only one Melanie had befriended, Gabrielle felt it was up to her to return the favor. How she was going to accomplish this, however, eluded her as the train pushed out onto the western desert.

Kelton crept ever closer and Gabrielle's heart beat a rapid staccato each time she thought of her arrival there. Before she was mentally ready, the news butch came through the car calling, "Kelton in five minutes."

Jordan opened his eyes and stretched his good hand and arm. "Why are you sitting stiff as a board? He'll like you, don't worry. There are so few single women out here, you'd be welcome if you were an old crone."

His attempt to reassure her was less that satisfactory. All she could think of was what she would do if Mr. Bailey didn't want her. And she couldn't come up with a single idea.

"What if he doesn't like me?" she asked Jordan in a voice barely above a whisper.

He reached across and took her hand. "He'll like you. He's probably pacing the platform worrying that you won't like him and wondering what he'll do if you don't." He smiled and gave her hand a reassuring pat.

The blast of the whistle announced their arrival and the train made its usual slamming, banging, grinding stop, to the discomfort of all. Gabrielle wondered if Melanie would appear to say goodbye or if she had already prepared for bed, since it was late. Gabrielle did want to see her once more.

A number of people got off, leaving the car nearly empty. "I haven't noticed this many people leave the train at one stop," she commented to Jordan.

"Probably going to catch the stage north into Idaho and Montana just like you and me." He stood up and stretched again. "Got your dolls?"

Gabrielle nodded and arranged the packages so she would have a free hand. "Think we'll see Melanie?"

"I doubt it. She's probably curled up in bed, licking her wounds, and hating me for them."

He held the heavy outside door for her and then followed her down the steps and out onto the dimly lit platform. She leaned into the wind that swept and eddied the unceasing dust into her face and mouth. Her eyes burned so she could hardly see, and there was such a crowd, she couldn't begin to pick out Mr. Bailey even if she had known what he looked like.

Gabrielle felt suddenly bewildered and frightened as she stood in the midst of the swirling crowd. Everyone else seemed to know exactly where they were going and what to do. She had no idea even how to claim her baggage.

A firm hand grasped her elbow and steered her forward toward the train depot. "If you'll stay inside where I can find you and watch my portfolio, I'll attend to the luggage." Jordan propelled her through an open door and into a long, narrow, smoke-filled room with a counter running its length. Along the opposite wall stood untidy groups of mismatched chairs, scarred but sturdy, clustered about numerous spittoons. He seated her in a chair near the door and placed the portfolio at her feet. "Give me your claim checks," he instructed and held out his hand to receive them.

Gabrielle placed the packages in the empty chair next to her, thus freeing both hands to locate the checks in the bottom corner of her purse. "I have three pieces," she said, handing him the precious claims.

He nodded and left her to scan what she could see of the platform through the open door, hoping to glimpse a man who appeared to be looking for someone. He had said he was reasonably tall with dark hair and a dark moustache. Unfortunately, that description fit at least half the men who walked past the door. She wanted to jump up and rush over to each one to inquire if he might be Mr. Bailey.

Instead, she sat very primly with her gloved hands folded in her lap and her feet crossed at the ankles, vaguely aware of the teeming activity of the trainmen as they filled the boilers with water, unloaded baggage and mail, and shunted cars to a siding. While she gave every indication of traveling alone and was situated visibly just inside the door, none of the men seemed to be looking for anyone. Nearly everybody, though, gave her a quick appraisal, to her great discomfort. Remembering what Jordan had said about the scarcity of women, she felt like she was on display and being evaluated before the bidding began.

Oh, Lord. Please stay close and help me. I haven't prayed much for my own needs, ever. But now I'm truly frightened, and I need Your comfort and strength to see me through. Amen.

She looked up to see Jordan following a strapping young man loaded with bags. "Set them right here next to the lady," Jordan commanded, and moving the chairs into further disarray with his foot, cleared a spot for their luggage.

"Stay near. We may need you to get us to the hotel." Jordan handed the boy a tip large enough to cause his eyes to light up.

"Yes, sir! I'll be real handy should you need me," he promised.

"Any sign of your man?" Jordan asked as he sank into the chair nearest hers.

"I can't tell, because I don't know what he looks like."

Jordan turned and looked at her through squinted eyes. "Not at all?"

"Vaguely, but the description fits so many of the men I've seen."

"What's his name and where's he live?"

"Edward Bailey from Marsh Creek."

Jordan hoisted himself from the chair and sauntered over to the counter. "Any word left here by an Ed Bailey of Marsh Creek?"

The stationmaster reset the green shade over his eyes and Gabrielle could hear the rustle of papers. Looking up, his face a sickly cast from the reflection, he shrugged, "Nope, not a thing."

Jordan nodded a thanks and returned to slouch back into the chair. The train sounded its whistle, a long eerie blast distorted by the wind, signaling its departure.

"There goes Melanie. I hope she'll be all right," Gabrielle said.

"Don't worry about her. She's got more lives than a cat. Just got blinded this trip. Happens once in awhile, even to the best."

They watched the train move slowly out of the station and then pick up speed. Gabrielle couldn't sit longer and moved to stand on the platform, looking until the train became only a faint moving light across the distant desert. Now the platform was deserted, save for the trainmen who were finishing their duties and the boy Jordan had paid to stay about in case they needed him. There was no one who stood as though searching for a lost passenger.

A great wave of despair rolled over Gabrielle. Whatever would she do now? She turned toward the station door as Jordan rose to his feet and motioned to the watching boy. "Let's take these bags to the best hotel. Which one do you recommend?"

"One over yonder. It's away from the stock corrals, and wind don't catch the dust so bad there."

"Much obliged. Think they'll have rooms? Seemed like a big crowd tonight."

"Always rooms if you got the money to pay for the best. It's the cheap ones goes first and the hands sleep four, five deep," he said.

They walked through the white powdery dust toward a two-storied wooden building with a wide false front, the front having been built in a futile attempt to create a bit of elegance. "Miners and cowboys don't pay no never-mind long as it's got a roof and a floor," he concluded as they entered the still brightly lit lobby.

While Jordan proceeded to the desk, Gabrielle looked about. It was far from the cleanliness she was used to back home, but the wooden planked floor had been swept and the plain pine furniture dusted rather recently.

The jingle of a key on a large ring made her realize she had left the securing of her room up to Jordan. She rushed to the desk and the clerk shoved the key ring into her hand.

"Down the hall. Last room on the right. Bath's two doors down on the left. The gentleman's directly across the hall."

She fumbled in her purse for her money. "What do I owe?"

"All been taken care of, 'cept you need to sign the register." He turned it around and handed her a fresh-dipped pen.

Quickly she signed her name. "The gentleman isn't paying for my accommodations. Please tell me the amount."

"For Pete's sake, Gabby, shut up. The stage leaves at six in the morning. It's late and I'm tired. Let's argue tomorrow. We'll have all day to settle it."

He stalked off down the hall without a backward glance, the young baggage handler close behind. Gabrielle, her face growing hot from his inelegant rebuff, had no choice but to follow. She had learned that Jordan in this mood was like an angered bull. Besides, tomorrow she would be rescued from his coarse manners and surly behavior by Mr. Bailey. She could endure much by keeping that thought foremost in her mind.

Jordan unlocked his room and watched as she finally managed to make the lock respond to her key. She searched for what she hoped was a proper tip while her three bags were being deposited inside her room. Jordan, however, peeled a bill off the roll he had won from Melanie and the boy snatched it eagerly.

"Be here at five-thirty. Wake us and carry our bags. Can you do that?" Jordan's voice was cold and demanding.

"Be here any time you say!" he said eagerly and ran quickly down the hall toward the front door.

Jordan, without looking at Gabrielle, shut his door and she could hear the springs of the bed groan under the weight of his body. His shoulder must be hurting badly again. Even the dim lamp on the wall showed the scar on the side of his face, and his skin had the gray pallor she had grown to expect.

Shutting her door, she took off her hat and gloves and laid them together with her purse on the once elegant oak dresser. Peering between the cracks in the mirror, she tucked some escaped locks of hair back under the heavy net and noticed a black smudge on her cheek. Whatever would Mr. Bailey think if he saw her so untidy. Wide, frightened eyes stared back at her. And what would she do if Mr. Bailey didn't come? Her hands began to shake at the thought and she willed further speculation to cease.

Taking the large china pitcher, hand-painted with yellow roses, from its matching wash basin, she slipped into the hall. The hour was so late the bath was empty, and she quickly filled the pitcher.

As she tiptoed passed Jordan's room on her return trip, she heard a soft moan. Knowing she wouldn't be able to sleep without at least offering help, she knocked softly on his door.

"Gabby?" the hoarse voice asked.

He hadn't locked the door and she pushed it open. A slice of light from the hall cut into the dark room, and she saw that he lay diagonally across the too-short bed, fully dressed. After pouring the cool water into the basin on the bedside table, she moistened a washcloth and wiped his face. Gently dabbing him dry, she changed the water and washed his hands. Unbuttoning the ridiculous-looking shirt he had worn all day, she peeled it back and, sitting beside him, gave him a sponge bath. He allowed her to cleanse him but made no verbal acknowledgment of her presence.

"I'm going to go for some carbolic acid crystals and

warm water. I'll be right back." The bed gave a hideous screech as she stood up.

He chuckled ever so softly. "Wonder if we're keeping our neighbors awake?"

"The wallpaper is probably all that divides the rooms," she whispered with a smile before she left for the supplies.

She ran her errand quickly and walked quietly back into his room. As she renewed the dressing she noted that the wound was healing well, but it was still tender. "Did you forget and try moving your arm?" she asked softly.

"Uh-huh. Dumb, wasn't it?"

"Just natural. Will you let me give you some laudanum tonight? I have a bottle in my case."

"No. I'll manage."

Even in the shadowed light, she could see his face still had the pallor and drawn lines signifying that he was in pain. "Why do you refuse relief and choose to suffer? Is it a penance you do?"

"No!" he snapped.

His abrupt answer seemed to end the conversation, and she quickly cleaned up her mess. If she kept her distress locked tightly away, she might get a bit of rest before the early wake-up time.

Apparently sensing she was about to leave, he asked, "Could I have a drink of water?"

She poured him a glass from the spare pitcher she had taken care to fill, and held it for him.

"Thanks," he breathed as he lay back down. "And thanks for braving the lion's den and coming in. I thought I could handle the pain, but it got worse instead of better after I lay down."

"I still don't understand why you won't take some painkiller," she pursued. "It's not like the little bit you've had is going to cause an addiction."

"That's what a doctor told me once, many years ago, but he was wrong. Oh, how wrong he was."

Jordan's face took on a bitter look that reflected in his voice, even as softly as he spoke.

Gabrielle, overwhelmed by his confession and having witnessed the agonies of drug withdrawal, knelt on the floor at his bedside and gently stroked his forehead. Without asking his permission, she prayed, "Dear Lord. Please hear me. Let this man's pain be soothed that he may rest the night. And if the pain must be, then let it be no more than he can bear. Amen."

As she continued to kneel and stroke his brow, she felt him relax and his breathing deepened. She stayed until she was sure he was asleep, then slipped noiselessly across the hall to her own room.

There was so little time before morning, it seemed foolish to remove her clothes. Unbuttoning her shoes and taking off her jacket, she stretched across the bed, closed her eyes, and pictured Jordan's peaceful, sleeping face until exhaustion overcame her.

CHAPTER 9

WHY WERE SOME PEOPLE so inconsiderate when others were so tired and needed to sleep? She rolled over and tried to pull the covers up around her chilly shoulders. There were no blankets, and the knocking persisted at the door. She snapped her eyes open and sat up, dazed.

"Ma'am, are you awake?" a male voice whispered.

"She may not be," a deep, gravelly voice boomed from the adjoining room, "but the rest of us are. Now shut up, boy, and get out of here 'fore I break you in half!"

"Ma'am?" A tone of desperation filled the boy's call.

In an overwhelming rush, Gabrielle realized where she was. "Yes, yes, I'm up. Thank you," she assured him and was answered by the sound of his footsteps retreating rapidly down the hall. The bed in the room next to hers creaked as the occupant turned over, obviously planning to go back to sleep. She could even hear the rustle of the bedclothes and the little grunting noises he made as he rearranged them.

Snores and night coughs echoed through her room as through a dormitory. She had the urge to touch the wall to see if it really existed, for if it did, the only thing it provided was privacy from peeping eyes.

In the moonlight that filled the room she sat staring at the wallpaper; its large paisley-like pattern was ugly beyond imagining. What was that dark smudge, approximately eye level, on the wall opposite her bed? Moving cautiously from the groaning bed, she walked across the room and touched it. It was a hole! Putting her eye to the spot, she could see plainly into the adjoining room. Could look right at the bed where a full-bearded hulk of a man slept. *So much for privacy.*

She dropped onto an old rickety chair, feeling terribly worn and forsaken, ready to cry. Then, slowly she sank to her knees. Lack of privacy prevented her from speaking aloud, so she prayed a silent prayer. *Lord, I'm truly at Your mercy. I am at everyone's mercy. I have no idea what to do, but I feel I must try to find the children for Ellen's sake. I shall try to stay very near You today so that I may hear the still, small voice and follow Your guidance. Amen.*

Then she stood, found the lamp, and lit it. The dim flickering light through the dirty chimney sent bizarre shadows dancing about the room. After pulling down the window blind, she located her shoes and sat gingerly on the unstable chair to put them on. She wanted no more to do with the loudly protesting springs of that bed.

Unpinning her hair, she brushed each dusty strand thoroughly. Then, before twisting it up, she washed her face vigorously with the cool water. Inspecting her image in the dull shards of mirror, made even more shadowy by the poor light, she had never seen such a sight as greeted her. The long days and sleepless nights had taken a fearful toll. Translucent skin stretched tight over wide, distraught eyes and sagged into mauve-colored pouches below. Long curved lines set her mouth in parentheses, and the flowing untamed hair created a perfect frame for the ruins. She felt and looked old, very old indeed. Why had everything conspired against her when she wanted, needed to look her best?

With a sigh, she quickly twisted her hair into its familiar chignon and secured it in the hair net. She replaced her hat and anchored it with three hatpins against the eternal wind she could hear whistling around and through the corner of the building.

She gave her jacket a vigorous dust-evicting shake and had her arms raised for a second flip when a deep sigh and an accompanying groan issued from her unhappy neighbor. She gave up and slipped it on, dust-filled and wrinkled. A soft knock on her door interrupted the buttoning of her jacket. "Yes," she whispered through the door without opening it.

"Ready?" Jordan's voice asked.

Her hand flew to her cheek. What caustic remark would he make when he saw her? Maybe if she kept her head tipped so the hat hid much of her face, she could escape his acid tongue.

Setting her shoulders preparatory to enduring whatever awaited her on the other side of the door, she tried to turn the key softly in the lock, but everything in this building seemed to squeak or rattle. A loud groan and grinding of springs from the next room let her know she had succeeded in disturbing its occupant again. She gave up trying to be quiet and swung the door open, letting the hinges creak as they would.

Jordan looked remarkably refreshed, and he had somehow even managed to get his hair neatly combed. A slightly crooked grin appeared as he carefully scrutinized her features, but he didn't speak, a fact for which she was grateful. Continuing grunts and moans from behind the wallpaper made her wish to be away as quickly as possible before further irritation roused the half-beast next door to action they would all regret.

Jordan tipped his head as a signal for the eager boy to claim her luggage. She pulled her cape around her shoulders and slipped on her gloves as they walked down the hall and out into the chilly, wind-whipped morning.

Jordan set his tan felt, wide-brimmed hat on his head, pulled it down over his eyes, and bent his body against the wind. He reached out and pulled her against him, using his body as a shield for her.

"We don't have time for much breakfast. Coffee'll have to do until we get to the first stage stop," he shouted.

"Fine," she answered, but the wind drove the word back down her throat and she wasn't sure he even heard.

She was terribly grateful he knew where he was going, for each time she looked up, the alkali dust blinded her. All she could do was clutch his hand, and since her full skirt and cape made a sail trying to carry her back the way they had come, she let him pull her forward in what she guessed was the direction of the stage station.

"Step up," he commanded.

She opened her eyes and found they were standing in front of another battered old building like so many she had seen the past few days. Stepping inside out of the wind-freshened air, she nearly smothered under the layers of cooking and tobacco smoke. Jordan led her through the haze to a small table, and he and the boy took the luggage to the counter.

Gabrielle watched him purchase tickets and go back outside. She guessed he wanted to supervise the loading of their things onto the stage coach. She wondered how much the ticket to Marsh Basin was, so she claimed the table with her gloves and went to the counter to ask.

"Ten dollars," came the brief answer. "Want to buy one?"

"N—n—no," she stammered. "Mine has been purchased."

The station master dismissed her with a curt nod and turned to someone more profitable.

She wouldn't make a scene here, but as Jordan had reminded her last night, they would have all day in which to settle their financial matters. She did not intend to have him paying her way as though she were a charity case, which, thanks to him, she wasn't.

The waiter set glasses of water on the table and returned with a pitcher of coffee and some mugs. "Cream or sugar?" he asked.

"Neither, thank you." She poured two steaming mugs full. Stirring them both, she attempted to cool the coffee enough to drink before the driver decided it was time to leave.

She watched Jordan return and pay the boy. Then, folding himself into the too-small chair, he reached for a mug.

Feeling better with the warm brew inside her, Gabrielle spread her purse on the table. "I would appreciate it if we could settle our debts before we proceed," she began.

"What debts you talking about?"

"Last night's room and the stagecoach ticket."

"Your pay for extra services rendered."

"I've given you no extra service," she objected.

"I call taking care of me last night when you were so tired you could scarcely move, extra service."

She moved her hand further into her purse in search of her money pouch.

"Gabby, don't make a scene. I won't take your money. You've earned every dime I've paid you, whether in money or goods. You don't know what you're going to find when you get to Marsh Basin." Then his eyes took on a slight twinkle. "Someday, when you're independently wealthy and want to do a good deed, start an orphanage or build a church in my name. That'll repay your debt to me.''

She laughed in spite of her burdens.

Jordan's eyes left her face. ''Hurry, finish your coffee,'' he urged. ''We're ready to board.''

She looked up to see the back of the driver as he disappeared out the door. Grabbing her purse and gloves, she darted headlong out the door and into the wind, letting it blow her to the stagecoach. The driver gave her a hand up into the Concord-style coach where she had her pick of the seats. There were four leather upholstered seats, two pairs facing each other, accommodating twelve passengers. This arrangement forced half the travelers to ride backward and since she was going the full day's travel, a fifty-mile distance, she quickly chose a front-facing seat in the corner of the back row.

Jordan clambered in and sprawled down beside her. She wondered if he ever sat up properly in a seat. When he approached a chair or couch, he reminded her of a puppet whose strings suddenly went slack. Today, his formless slouching would uncomfortably crowd the people sitting next to him, one of which was she. She anticipated a most uncomfortable trip even if the road was smooth, and that wasn't likely. She decided to wait a few minutes until the space appeared needed, however, before suggesting he sit closer to her lest he read something improper into her motive.

She watched the coach fill rapidly with an intriguing group of people. There were two Indians wrapped in bright red blankets who chose the seats opposite her, several cowboys and miners, two men conspicuous in their city clothes, and a well-dressed elderly couple. All the seats were filled except the one on which she and Jordan sat.

Still the coach didn't move. They must be waiting

for the one missing passenger. Then she heard voices outside discussing where someone was going to sit. If that person was to have any room at all, Jordan was going to have to sit up. He made no sign that he planned to do so.

Much as she hated saying anything, the time had come. "Jordan, you'll have to make room for the last passenger."

"Do you see anyone looking for a seat?"

"Not at the moment, but since the driver hasn't mounted his seat, and the people outside are discussing the seating, it seems most likely."

In a voice intended to halt further discussion of the issue, Jordan informed her, "There aren't any more passengers."

Was he trying to intimidate her? "You say that with such authority. What gives you superior knowledge?"

He gave a low chuckle. "I learned to count at a very early age."

"I, too, had the advantage of an excellent education. Therefore, unless my eyesight is failing, I count only eleven people."

"You are exactly right. However, there were twelve tickets sold."

His face held such a smug look, she longed for some way to erase it. However, her insatiable curiosity made her ask the question she knew he was aching to answer. "How do you know that?"

"I bought two."

"Two! Why would you spend twenty dollars for two tickets?"

"For precisely the reason you have observed. There isn't much room and with my size and injured shoulder, I don't propose to be packed like a pickle in a barrel. I plan to indulge myself and travel in a bit of comfort. Ever ridden any distance on a stagecoach?"

"No. Just wagons and buggies and, of course, the train."

"It'll be a different experience. You'll appreciate the extra room before six o'clock tonight," he predicted. "Unless, of course, you'd rather trade places with one of the other passengers and be spared riding with me." The tilt of his head and the twist of his mouth seemed to dare her to move.

She might have considered his suggestion, but when she looked at the other choices, she decided sharing the bench with Jordan was preferable. Refraining from comment on his last statement, she chose, rather, to sit silently staring out the window at the side of the stage station. It was a colorless blot in the light from the large candles covered with a dome of glass attached to the coach. This was the light by which they would travel until daybreak. The flickering flames seemed almost worse than no light, for they cast huge undulating shadows that distorted everything.

A loud thump above Gabrielle's head indicated a late piece of luggage had just been loaded, and she heard the driver tell someone he could ride in the dickey seat.

"What's a dickey seat?" She couldn't resist asking Jordan.

"A little seat behind the driver. Use it if they have an overload."

They continued to wait. "What's the matter now?"

"Got a heavy load. Probably having to hitch up another team or two. You gettin' eager to meet your man?"

"Mr. Bailey isn't 'my man.'" She denied the statement vehemently even though the words appealed mightily to her. "I am getting anxious, however, to see my nieces and stop traveling. I don't seem cut out for the vagabond life. I enjoy my own possessions around me, well-prepared food, and cleanliness."

Jordan's answer was cut short by a whistle and

shout from the driver. The horses responded instantly and the coach rolled north out of Kelton toward the Idaho Territory and Marsh Basin.

Unlike the sideways motion of the train, the stagecoach rode with a rocking motion from front to back, and Gabrielle felt she was in danger of being thrown into the lap of the taciturn Indian sitting in front of her. He, however, braced his moccasined foot hard against the floor and withdrew into his blanket.

Along the eastern horizon, mountain ridges stood, flat black silhouettes against the faint cream-colored light of dawn. Not the imperiously rugged peaks of the Wasatch Mountains between Ogden and Salt Lake City, but softer in their contours.

Even with the extra room, the leg space was inadequate for Jordan's long limbs, so his knees spraddled sideways, brushing against Gabrielle's skirts. She withdrew into her corner as far as possible and kept her feet primly together and her hands in her lap, elbows tucked tightly against her ribs. They hit a bump and his knee swayed over and collided with her. From the corner of her eye she could see his head turn in her direction and a slow smile spread over his face.

She sat stiff and silent, staring straight ahead, giving no indication anything untoward had occurred. At last, giving his bearded stubble an absent-minded scratching, he turned and gazed out at the scenery without saying a word.

The sun popped from behind the distant east mountains into a cloudless sky and lit the valley along which they traveled. Ahead she could see an unimposing rise of peaks. As they neared the foothills the shrubbery thickened and Jordan raised his arm, silently pointing. She sighted a line down his finger to where a cottontail raced for cover under a clump of sagebrush. She kept her eyes riveted to the spot until they reached and passed it, then eagerly cast about, searching for more animal life. A huge bird appeared out the window on Jordan's side, circling high over the desert valley.

"A hawk," Jordan informed her. "Here, scoot over so you can see it better."

Taking care not to jostle his injured shoulder, she bent to see from his window the soaring flight as the hawk searched for breakfast. Finally, it disappeared and she returned to her own corner.

After fifteen miles, they pulled into a log stage station built against the mountain. Here they could eat and stretch their legs while the lathered, sweat-drenched team that had pulled them this far was led away and fresh horses hitched in their places.

Jordan got out first and reached up a brown hand to help her down. Startled, she stared at it, quite unprepared for this act of civility from him.

"Don't bump your head," he warned. "Door's not made for people our size."

She bent nearly double to get through, almost tripped on her skirt, and grasped Jordan's steadying hand, grateful for its support. She had thought the dust on the train was bad, but it was mild compared to that raised by eight horses and the heavy coach. After examining her suit, she didn't dare imagine what her face must look like. Her mouth and teeth felt grainy and tasted slightly salty. She spit out the first mouthfuls of water she drank from the long-handled dipper provided together with the community water bucket.

Gabrielle ached for a hot soaking bath, freshly laundered clothes, and a full, newly plumped eider-down mattress. She was beginning to wonder if she was cut out for life in such a savage environment. The only hope she held was that Ellen had apparently not only endured, but enjoyed life on their ranch. And since Ellen was not the pioneering type, this must indicate that things would improve after she arrived in Marsh Basin. These were the thoughts she dwelled on as the day droned by.

From the cold of the morning to a comfortable forenoon temperature, the afternoon turned distressingly warm so that she was forced to remove first her cape and then her jacket.

"You'd feel even cooler if you'd take off those infernal gloves," Jordan said.

She scowled at him. They and her hat were the last vestiges of civilized dress left, and she had no intention of parting with them. She clasped her gloved hands in her lap and turned her head to stare out her window, or rather watch the dust roll in through it.

By the time they reached Connor Creek, the last stop for fresh horses before starting up the summit and down into Marsh Basin, Gabrielle's resolve to wear the gloves had wilted as the heat increased. She now removed them and jammed them into her purse, refusing to look in Jordan's direction as she did so.

During the last miles of the trip, she was too tired even to fret about what she would do if Mr. Bailey failed to meet the stage in Marsh Basin or if he was there, what he would think, seeing her so disheveled and travel-stained. If he wasn't there, she had enough money for a hotel room and a bath. It would be dark by the time the stage arrived, and they couldn't travel to the ranch tonight, anyway. She was guaranteed a hot bath, no matter what.

"Marsh Basin coming up, folks," the driver hollered. "Whoa! whoa!" he bellowed at the teams, and the stagecoach rattled and rocked to its final stop of the day.

"Sorry, we're a bit late getting in," the driver apologized as he opened the coach door.

Although the sun had set only recently behind the hills, the temperature drop was amazing. Gabrielle buttoned her jacket and took the wadded lump of gloves from her purse. They were still wet from the perspiration that had forced their removal. She stared at them ruefully and then re-deposited them back inside the purse.

126

"Atta girl. Make a westerner out of you yet," Jordan said.

"If going about gloveless makes me a westerner, then I shall never be classed as such," she retorted. "It is only because my others are packed that I am in this predicament. I only hope Mr. Bailey is tolerant."

"Oh, I hope he is, too." The sarcasm fairly dripped from Jordan's voice.

She glared at him, but he failed to see her. He had turned his back on her and was crouching through the doorway. The coach creaked its protest as Jordan stepped outside. This time, however, he walked off, leaving her to manage by herself. The driver noticed her struggle and came to her rescue.

"Thank you very much. Even after the several opportunities today, I fear I haven't mastered a graceful way to dismount," she said.

"Little kids is the only ones I ever seen get out without problems. That's why I drive the coaches. Wouldn't ride inside lessen I was trussed up at gunpoint." He grinned at her and held on to her hand just a fraction longer than was necessary.

Gabrielle slid her hand from his palm. "Thank you for your assistance."

He threw the bag of mail over his shoulder and fell into step beside her. "Got someone meetin' you?"

"Mr. Edward Bailey," she answered briefly, not because she wished to be rude, but because she was too tired to carry on a conversation.

He held the door to the station open for her, and she entered a duplicate of the ones she had seen at each stop. In the flickering lamplight, she could scarcely recognize Jordan as he claimed his luggage. How would she know Mr. Bailey whom she had never seen?

However, she needn't have worried. The driver solved her problem. "Edward Bailey here?" his voice boomed over the hubbub in the room. There was no response to his question. "Anyone know an Edward Bailey?" Again, only silence greeted his query.

Gabrielle felt her knees grow weak, and she groped for a chair. A strong firm arm circled her waist and guided her over to the station counter. "Lean on this while I get your bags," Jordan ordered.

Perhaps it was just as well Mr. Bailey hadn't come. This would give her an opportunity to recover her poise and be ready to face the uncertainties tomorrow was sure to bring. She was dimly aware of Jordan making arrangements for hotel rooms and baths and, when he took her elbow, she offered no resistance as he guided her from the stage station and out along a dusty road.

They walked in silence, their way lighted by the lingering afterglow of the departed sun. A slight raise of her elbow signaled her to step up and together, they entered the lobby of the Marsh Basin Hotel. It was far from elegant, but Gabrielle only asked a hot bath and four walls without spying holes.

Scraping, banging sounds behind her caused her to turn around and there she saw a rotund, bearded man of undecipherable age puffing for breath under the load of bags he was toting. He apparently was trying to bring as much luggage in one trip as he could carry.

Jordan deposited Gabrielle in a chair and attended to the registering. She didn't wish to be further beholden to him, but at the moment she had no strength with which to assert her independence. The baggage man stood, his giant chest heaving, waiting for his tip.

Gabrielle, facing the door, watched the lobby begin filling with customers and the stage driver come swinging through carrying of all things, Jordan's portfolio. *Why would he have that?* she wondered numbly. Jordan never let it out of his protection.

Jordan turned around and left the desk, two large key rings hanging over the hand on his injured arm.

128

He tipped the portly baggage man for his trouble and started in Gabrielle's direction.

The driver stepped up and intercepted him. "Here's your portfolio, Mr. Cooke," the driver said. "You left before we got the express box opened, and I figured you might want this tonight."

"Thanks," Jordan said, and started to hand the driver a tip.

He brushed Jordan's hand away. "Keep your money. I ain't no servant. Warn't no bother. Comin' over here anyways. They gettin' you folks fixed up?" He nodded toward Gabrielle. "Hope her man comes for her tomorrow. The lady looks near done in and could stand a mite 'o tendin'."

Jordan turned and looked carefully at her. She must look awful and she bowed her head to hide her face. Now, at least, all he could see was the top of her hat.

Not looking at him, she was unaware he had bent over until he spoke softly in her ear. "There's a hot bath waiting for you in your room. You can soak as long as you like."

She looked up into his face and couldn't resist smiling. "Did you know it would take bribery to get me to move?"

"I figured it might," he said, and a smile lit his tired features.

After they found their rooms, the baggage man unscrambled their cases and finally deposited the right ones in each room. Gabrielle scarcely noticed his problem, however, for there in the middle of a clean room sat a portable brass bathtub filled with hot water. The sight so delighted her she very nearly burst into tears. She turned to close the door and met Jordan's smiling face, apparently enjoying her rapture at the anticipation of her first bath in a week.

"When you've soaked to your heart's content and are dressed, we'll have dinner. The food here is excellent, and I've ordered something special."

Stated as an order, as was nearly everything else he said, she was irritated and wanted to tell him she wasn't hungry . . . he could eat his specially ordered meal by himself. However, she was too hungry and practical to turn down such a tempting suggestion—especially when it sounded like the first digestible fare in days.

She nodded and started to close the door. Across the hall, his door stood open and she could see into his room where a duplicate of her tub stood ready for him. It suddenly crossed her mind that he would be unable to untie his sling or unwrap his bandages.

"I'll undo your wrappings. I made an extra set which is in your travel bag. When you're finished bathing, I'll renew your dressings."

It took only a few minutes to remove his shirt and to unwind the strips, now gray with dust-caked perspiration. He stood before her, naked from the waist up, trim and lean, his statuesque body only marred by the large healing gash across the muscles of the right shoulder and upper arm. Obviously a man used to hard, physical work, and yet he remained maddeningly vague about his occupation. Even through her exhaustion, she found his unclothed presence disturbing to her. Since she had seen him thus numerous times and usually felt no attraction, she became highly annoyed at her reaction. As she had previously, she rationalized that she was transferring her long-expected meeting with Mr. Bailey to Jordan. The mixed emotions of disappointment at Mr. Bailey's not meeting the stage and relief that he wouldn't see her looking so disheveled must be causing her to be affected. So thinking, she left, bidding him goodbye with a silent nod.

CHAPTER 10

A SMALL CRACKLING FIRE in the little Lady Franklin
stove had driven the chill from her bedroom, making
it toasty and inviting. Gabrielle opened one of the
suitcases and took out a bar of special Castile soap
and set it by the tub. The pungent homemade lye soap
furnished by the hotel would remove not only the dirt
but a couple of layers of skin as well.

Before undressing, however, she made a thorough
inspection of the white calcimine-painted walls. She
didn't want to fret all the while she was in the tub
about someone watching through a peephole from
another room. Satisfied that she had complete privacy, the first in days, she disrobed, all the while
keeping her eyes glued to the steaming tub as though
it was a mirage that might suddenly disappear.

She tested the temperature with her big toe. Much
as she hated to, she was forced to pour in a pitcher of
cold water. Now she was able to inch her way in until
all but her head was submerged and her knees, bent in
the air because her legs were too long to stretch out if
the rest of her body was to soak. How lovely it felt to

lie back and relax completely, to know she owed no one any service, and didn't have to get out until she chose.

A board creaked overhead. Slowly she opened her eyes. Looking at her bright pink skin and wrinkled fingertips, she knew she must have dozed off. Then a horrible thought stirred through her lethargic mind. She turned her eyes to the ceiling and scrutinized it carefully. There seemed to be no marks, however, that would have indicated an observation hole from above.

Thus reassured, she soaped the washrag and scrubbed away the final dirt that hadn't soaked off. Her hair was now the biggest problem. It was stiff and gray with dust. If she washed it, though, how would she get it dry in time for dinner tonight? And she was getting very hungry. Remembering Jordan's promise of a special meal triggered voracious responses in her stomach.

The fire! There was extra wood. She could heat the stove up again with a couple of sticks and brush her hair dry in front of it. Quickly, she stepped from the tub out onto a towel laid especially to catch the drips and vigorously rubbed herself dry. Reviving the fire, she then knelt with her head over the tub and using the fresh water from the pitchers, gave herself a much-needed shampoo.

Oh, her hair felt so good and perhaps, if she was lucky, the road to the ranch wouldn't be too dusty, and it would stay clean for a while. After drying the long strands, she wrapped her head in a towel, turban-style, and slipped on her undergarments.

She put a heavy layer of skin cream over her face and turned her attention to the hair. Gabrielle's hair was fine and so, with careful combing and brushing as she bent her head to catch the heat from the little stove, it was soon dry. The heat also helped the cream to absorb, and as she parted her hair in the middle and coiled it into the usual controlled knot, she couldn't help noticing how refreshed she looked. Maybe she wouldn't scare witches at Halloween, after all. She decided to leave the hair net off and even pulled a few tiny strands from the stern roll at the back of her head, allowing them to curl in wispy ringlets around her ears and along her neck as she had seen Melanie do.

The softer hairdo made her feel so elegant, she wished she had a special dress for the occasion. All she owned, though, were practical calicos and two dark skirts and three blouses. She donned a black skirt and a pastel yellow silk blouse. She closed the loops over the long row of buttons on the deep cuffs and up the front of the bodice, then stretched her neck and smoothed the tight lace up her throat until it almost touched her earlobes.

Using an old cloth, she polished the dust from her black leather shoes and sat on the bed to button them. She arranged a white and yellow crocheted shawl about her shoulders and took another peek in the mirror. She was no Melanie DeWitt, but she certainly looked better than she had for several days.

A knock at the door interrupted her appraisal. "You decent?" Jordan asked.

"Yes," she answered and hastened to unlock the door. She swung it open and found him lounging against the door jamb, the bandages dangling from his hand. His hair was a damp tangled mass, and his skin from the waist up glowed, still pink from his soak.

"I believe you offered to put these on," he said, and held the stack of cloth out to her.

"I seem to recall making such a rash agreement," she smiled.

He pushed past her and into the room. "Wait" she dashed in front of him and gathered her underthings which were still lying in a heap next to the tub.

He laughed. "I don't need sheltering. I've seen plenty of lacy undergarments."

She glared at him from over her shoulder, wrapping them inside the dirty travel duster she had rolled up inside her valise.

He sat down on the bed and waited for her. She laid her shawl across the bed and took a jar of healing salve from her case and began gently spreading some over the wound.

"What in thunderation's in that stuff," he bawled.

"Don't tell me it hurts because I'll know you're lying if you do." And she continued to apply it evenly about the gash.

"It's the smell, woman. I'm not going to live with that. Take it off!" he ordered.

"I will not take it off, and you will live with it. Soon you won't be able to smell the turpentine."

"But everyone near me will. And turpentine isn't all I can smell! Smells like a sheep camp!"

"That's the mutton tallow."

"And what other wonderful ingredients have you put in this witches' brew?"

"Witches' brew! You ingrate! This is an old family cure that's been used for generations."

"Smells like you're still on the first batch." He turned his head away and sulked.

"If you'd like to make a new batch, you add balm of Gilead buds to the turpentine and tallow," she offered sweetly and proceeded to bandage him back up.

She tied the final knot in the sling. "There. You're ready to do battle with whatever it is you fight." She screwed the lid back on the jar and bent over to return the salve to her bag.

"I fight with stubborn nurses, but I can't win. They rig the battles, and they never fight fair." His good humor had apparently returned.

She snapped the bag shut. "If we didn't, we'd be annihilated by the likes of you and then what would the world do?" She folded the damp towels and hung them over the back of a chair near the fire to dry.

"Stop fussing about and come here," he demanded.

Not feeling up to sparring more, she crossed the room and stood next to him, silently waiting to hear what it was he wanted.

"Are you in the mood to grant another favor?" he asked, his voice soft, imploring, but his eyes averted from her face.

She straightened like a bolt. What favor could he have in mind?

Forcing her voice to remain unemotional, she asked, "And what might that be, Mr. Cooke?"

He kept his head turned from her and seemed anxious not to look at her. This wasn't normal. He usually watched her face intently as though catching the panoply of emotions gave him pleasure.

He cleared his throat and fussed with the sling around his neck. "I know I have no right to ask more of you, but I'm willing to pay. I know you're tired and I don't expect your services for free. But my beard is causing great discomfort and I would pay dearly for relief."

"Then, perhaps we should use your room since all the shaving things are over there."

He stood and waited for her to proceed him.

At length, he was groomed to his satisfaction and they stopped by the room for her shawl and purse before proceeding to the dining room.

"Sure you haven't forgotten something?" he asked.

She looked in the mirror and checked her person carefully. "No, I don't think so," she said, puzzled.

"Do you mean you're going to be seen in public without your gloves?" He threw up his hand and looked shocked.

"Just for that, I should put some on," she said.

"Don't try," he said as he took her arm and hurried her out.

They arrived in a dining room not unlike all the others she had seen lately, full of unkempt hungry travelers eating family-style at large rectangular tables. Why had she pictured herself sitting at a handsomely set table for two in an intimate corner and being graciously served delicacies cooked to perfection?

A thin woman nearly as tall as Gabrielle came stalking through the room. "Right this way, Mr. Cooke." While her voice was pleasant enough, her face looked like it had been cast in plaster of Paris the moment after she tasted a lemon.

"Thanks, Mrs. Solomon," Jordan said.

Without a smile, she turned and walked toward a door on the far end of the long room. Jordan took Gabrielle's elbow and guided her slowly through the tables. The talk in the room suddenly grew hushed, and Gabrielle felt all eyes following her as she moved across the room. She grew terribly uncomfortable and appealed to Jordan for help.

"Smile," he whispered in her ear. "You're a treat these men don't often see. Give them some dreams for their pillows tonight."

She fixed what she hoped was a pleasant, not too large, smile and nodded at the tables as they sauntered past. Men half-rose from their tables in clumsy deference, reached to doff hats, and returned wide, delighted smiles at her.

So this was how it felt to be beautiful. No wonder women fought to save their looks. This was an exhilarating stimulant and experienced often enough, the desire for more could lead one to become foolish or even dangerous. By the time they reached the small private dining room, she felt a special glow, inside and out. She also knew the men weren't the only ones with dreams for their pillows tonight. She would not soon forget that feeling.

CHAPTER 11

MRS. SOLOMON WAITED PATIENTLY while Jordan seated Gabrielle at the small round table covered with a cream-white crocheted lace tablecloth, and set with fine hand-painted china, cut crystal, and sterling silver.

Their hostess lit the four tapers in the elaborate silver candelabra placed in the center of the table. "You can parade through my dining room every night if you'd like. Don't get many 'lookers' here. It'd sure be good for business."

There was no smile on the woman's face and Gabrielle didn't know if she was serious or not. However, the urge to giggle very nearly overcame Gabrielle as she pictured herself strolling through the dining room each evening, for the purpose of attracting business for the owner.

"I'll have your first course out in a minute," Mrs. Solomon said, and left the small room, being very careful to close the door.

Suddenly, Gabrielle felt unnaturally shy. Although she had heard detailed accounts of evenings like this from Ellen, she had never been entertained in such a manner. She became tongue-tied and her brain froze.

Jordan, apparently sensing her discomfort, leaned back casually in his chair and evaluated her. "You look absolutely ravishing this evening, Miss Sevier," he said, easy and reassuring.

Gabrielle, quickly recovering her poise and remembering the hostess's remark, smiled. "I'm so glad you noticed, Mr. Cooke. I thought my fabulous looks might go unobserved by you. Mrs. Solomon offered me a position here because of them, you know."

A grin played at the corners of Jordan's mouth. He sat forward a bit, took a long drink of water, all the while never taking his eyes from her face. He placed the goblet back on the table and twisted the stem slowly between his fingers. "Going to take it?"

She sighed dramatically. "It's tempting, but then when the looks are gone, you're out of luck. I'm hunting for something more permanent."

He edged the candlabra to one side and leaned forward, resting his forearm on the table. "Like being a wife and mother?"

Flustered by his direct knowing question, she attempted to cover her confusion with a brief laugh. "Oh goodness, nothing so mundane!" She fluttered her fingers in the air as she had seen the belles in Nashville do. "I was thinking more in the line of lady gambler. Such adventure, and Melanie tells me when the looks fade, one can always build a business establishment and go right on playing cards."

"I take it you don't approve."

"I don't, but I really am concerned about her. It seems to me you took an unreasonable advantage and left her in dire straits."

"She had fair warning, and she chose to ignore it."

"Did you need her money?"

"Money is the one thing in this world I don't need."

"Then, why did you not just tell her you wouldn't play her further?"

"Because she'd not have taken 'no' for an answer. She would have wheedled, then insulted, and finally appealed to the crowd, making me look like I did need the money because I refused to allow her to get even. I've known Melanie a lot of years, from riverboat to train. She'd have had those last games if there was any possible way."

Their cocktail, a delectable fruit cup, arrived. "Where did Mrs. Solomon get such delicious fruit?" Gabrielle asked when they were alone again.

"The old gal bottles a grocery store full of stuff and buys the rest by the case. Pay her enough and I think she'd find some way to import fresh fruit, too."

"You must have spent a great deal of time at this hotel to know so much."

"I've been in and out," he answered vaguely and gave his full attention to eating the fruit.

Gabrielle forced herself to eat slowly. Finished, she laid the spoon at the side of her plate and watched Jordan's attempt at manners while contending with his untrained hand. "You're becoming surprisingly adept with your left hand," she commented.

"I adjust rapidly to most situations."

"You speak of traveling a great deal. What kind of work do you do?"

"Anything that interests me." He finished and pushed the dish aside. Again leaning forward and resting on his arm, he said, "That's enough about me. Let's talk about you. Tell me more about your childhood."

"No," she said abruptly. "We are going to talk about you. Every time we broach the subject, you shift the conversation. I'd like to know about *your* childhood. Where were you born and what did you do as a child?"

There was a long pause. Mrs. Solomon removed the

empty cups and set steaming bowls of French onion soup in front of them. *This could be a quiet evening,* Gabrielle thought, but she was prepared to wait him out.

At last he spoke. His voice was distant and the sentences came out slowly, broken, as though he was having trouble putting the words together. "I was born and raised in a small town in southcentral Pennsylvania. My father taught English at a college there, and my mother gave piano lessons. I was an only child—pampered, adored, spoiled." He paused and looked up at her. "Enough?" His face remained shielded, but his eyes held a haunted look.

Perhaps in kindness to him, she should change the subject, but the puzzle was too complicated and intriguing. She desperately wanted to know more. "With a childhood like that, why is it so hard for you to talk about your home? I could understand if you'd been unwanted, or abused and starved."

"Because I haven't been back since I left in 1862." His voice was barely a whisper, and now he kept his head bowed.

Gabrielle could feel a terrible tension building. He hadn't been home since right after the War started. Why? What terrible secret did this man keep locked away? He must be close to telling her and now she was frightened. Did she really want to know?

Then he raised his head, and his voice, its normal deep rich baritone, broke into her thoughts. "Where were you born?" he asked casually, looking as though the preceding words hadn't been spoken.

Before she could answer, Mrs. Solomon entered and began serving the main course, wild duck in orange sauce. Gabrielle made small talk. "You were right about the food. The duck looks wonderful. Worth starving over half a continent for."

Gabrielle cut into her dinner and was enjoying the first bite, when she looked over at Jordan. His one-handed dining skills were taxed beyond their limit. "If you won't object, I'll cut your duck," she offered.

"It's either that, or I pick it up whole."

His eyes held a twinkle now, and she was relieved. It would have been a shame to spoil such a lovely meal. She prepared his main course, and the conversation died as they both ate.

Gabrielle finally set her fork beside the knife and proclaimed, "I've definitely had a sufficiency and it feels wonderful."

"Yes, doesn't it," he agreed. Now, he sat back from the table, relaxed, gazing at her. "While we wait for dessert, it's your turn to talk about yourself."

There was so much more she wanted to know about him, but he seemed determined to avoid discussing his past. Rather than risk his ire and ruin the evening, she recounted some amusing adventures of her youth.

He laughed heartily at her stories. "Where did all this nonsense take place?" he asked.

"I was born in a large plantation house in Franklin, Tennessee. It was a showplace until the War, then it became a hospital and I, out of necessity, became a nurse." She looked carefully at him. Something seemed to change, but she couldn't tell exactly what. Physically, he sat a bit straighter, tipped his head slightly so that his face was shadowed, and nervously began twisting a spoon. But there was more, a distinct difference in the atmosphere.

He moved his chair back slightly so that he sat out of the circle of candlelight. The air currents in the room caused the candles to flicker and smoke, casting giant demon-like shadows behind him. They danced, grotesque and eerie, weaving and undulating, as they wove their fiendish spells about him. Gabrielle, not normally given to imaginative flights of this magnitude, shivered imperceptibly. The altered mood between them remained and Gabrielle grew cold under its dominion.

They sat in silence while Mrs. Solomon cleared the table and brought dessert, small apple tarts with whipped cream. Gabrielle's hands lay in her lap, cold and stiff, so that when she moved to pick up her dessert fork, her fingers refused to function properly. She dropped the fork onto the polished pine wood floor with a clang that ripped through the charged room. Jordan jerked, nearly overturning his chair.

"Sorry," she murmured, and an uncomfortable knot formed in her throat, making it impossible to swallow.

She poked at the tart, attempting to look like she was eating. However, the effort was futile. At last, she gave up. "I'm too full. I can't seem to finish my dessert," she said lamely.

Jordan didn't answer her at once and it seemed impossible to make contact. What on earth had she said to bring about such a change?

Finally, he reached for her dish, but his eyes stayed just out of range of hers. "I'll eat the rest if you can't." His voice sounded natural enough, but his face was an emotionless blank, revealing nothing. "Mrs. Solomon doesn't take kindly to her food being wasted."

Gabrielle sat wordless in the heavy silence while he cleaned up the plate.

He returned the dish to her and pushed back his chair. "What would you like to do now?"

The question was asked casually enough, but in light of the past few minutes, she didn't quite know how to answer. She would like to step outside for a bit, but she didn't want to go alone. Since he apparently wasn't in a hurry to end the strained evening, she decided to answer him truthfully. "If it's not too cold and dark, I'd love to take a walk. It seems years since I've been able to stretch my legs."

Mrs. Solomon came into the room just then and began clearing the table. "This has been one of the most delicious meals I've ever eaten," Gabrielle said.

"You did yourself proud tonight," Jordan added. "Thanks."

"Glad to do it. Anytime."

It was amazing how such an agreeable person could look so out of sorts, Gabrielle thought, as she gathered her shawl around her shoulders and prepared to walk back through the dining room.

"There's a side door you can use if you like," Mrs. Solomon said, and pointed to the entrance she had been using.

"Shall we?" Jordan asked. "Or would you prefer to thrill the diners in the other room again?"

"O, they've seen enough for one night," Gabrielle said easily, and allowed Jordan to tuck her hand into the crook of his elbow.

A light breeze cooled her face as they stepped from the hotel. There was a near full moon and it lighted the roadway clearly. "You interested in sauntering or did you have some serious walking in mind?" Jordan asked.

"I have serious walking in mind. I feel cricked mentally and physically."

He slid her hand from his arm, and they started down the wagon road. He set a brisk pace, but she kept up well. They both finally became so breathless, however, they were forced to stop.

"Altitude does me in," he panted. "Takes awhile to get used to it when I come back." He found a smooth fallen log near the stream, and they sat down to rest.

When they were breathing easier, Jordan leaned back against a tree trunk and looked at her. "Let's hear some more of those interesting tales you tell."

"I'd really rather hear some of yours." She wondered if he would tell her what caused the tension at dinner.

His face was a blank and his eyes, shuttered. "I don't have a past, just a future. Since I haven't lived that yet, I can't tell you anything."

"I don't think it's the lack of a past. I think it's the checkered quality which discourages you from talking about it," she teased, attempting to lighten the heaviness between them.

"And you have no skeletons in your closet you'd rather not air?"

"Most certainly not!"

He closed his eyes, and his face took on a sad pensive look. "How lucky you are."

They sat again in silence, but Gabrielle's thoughts dwelt on his last remark. She also remembered the scars which she had assumed were from the War. Perhaps she had guessed wrong. "Want to talk about your skeletons?" she offered.

His mouth twisted into a tortured grin. "You sure you want to hear about them?"

"How would I know?"

"Because they have to do with the War, they're not pretty, and I haven't talked about them with anyone."

"That was years ago. Why have you waited so long?"

"Wasn't ever anyone around who cared, or who'd been there and knew what I was saying. You were there, and I know you cared."

Baffled at his references, she asked, "Where was I?"

"At Franklin, Tennessee."

Chills swept over her and she shivered involuntarily. "You were at Franklin?" she whispered.

"I'm that Yankee commander you vowed to hate absolutely and completely all the days of your life. The one who shot up your little boys, then sent them back to your big plantation house for you to put back together."

Her veins ran glacial as she stared at him. He looked at her now, his eyes cold and defiant, never wavering from her face.

She spoke in a whisper, but each word pinged on

144

the air like frozen ice crystals. "How do you know about the vow?"

Their eyes locked. "Because I heard it."

She pulled her shawl tight about her. "How?" she asked, but no sound came out.

"The shooting had stopped for the night. We were bedded down in the trees not far from your house, waiting for daybreak so we could march south." His voice was flat and lifeless, completely devoid of inflections. "You came out to the well, carrying an empty bucket. Someone in my outfit coughed, and you realized the woods were full of Yankees. A full moon lit you up like a spotlight. You turned and raised your arms above your head and shouted how you hated all of us, and would until the day we died."

Her voice recovered enough to speak aloud, she interrupted him. "I know what I shouted. The words have echoed in my head and heart ever since. I didn't realize how they had colored my every act until Doc reminded me on the train. And I wanted to kill him for that. Would have killed him if I'd had a weapon."

"I know. I felt it, and that's when I knew you were the one I'd seen that night in '65. I can also feel the hate leaving you. That's good. You can't possibly hate me as much as I hate myself, and you shouldn't let your little hate ruin your life."

"What do you mean, 'little hate'? I think I've carried a right good chunk."

"Couldn't match mine. Can't kill and maim boys and not feel it. And if you think you hate Yankees, I can tell you I match you in hatred for the South. How can a cause be so right that young boys would be sent, untrained, against veteran troops? Men slaughtering boys!" He spat the words and shuddered at the memory.

"But you did it," she accused.

"Yes, I did it. It isn't common combat practice to look the enemy in the eye and ask his age before

145

attacking. The third day, in the rain and standing ankle deep in mud, I saw what I was doing. Saw my bayonet sticking in the neck of a boy, not fourteen. Knew we'd won the war and killed all their men, so they sent us the young to massacre. I started to puke and I couldn't stop. I rode away from the battle, still puking my guts out, and I never went back. I still hear that boy's scream and relive that second when I plunged the knife into his throat. Then I look in his face and see he hasn't even shaved for the first time. I've killed a child!''

The restrained loathing underneath his words appalled her. And then those dreadful moments when she held him in her arms and tried to waken him flashed before her. ''Was that what you were dreaming that night on the train?''

''Yes.'' She sensed rather than heard his answer. He dropped his head and continued in a raw hoarse whisper. ''There's no way to pay for that, Gabby, except to give my life for his, and I'm too much of a coward. I go on living, praying someone else will put me out of my misery. But no one will kill me, and I don't die. You even came along when I had my best chance in years, prayed I'd recover, and saved me. I can't be free of the nightmare, no matter what.''

He shrank inside himself, cutting her off. The lonely hoot of a nearby owl sent chills through her shivering body. Not once over the years had it occurred to her that they weren't animals, unconscienced devils, who enjoyed wreaking that final havoc on the South. They were men with families, some with boys at home the same age as those they were facing on the battlefield. How many other Northern soldiers were eating themselves up with self-hate? And now she could see it wasn't any one individual's fault. They had, North and South, all been caught in a giant trap and survived to bear the guilt, the blame, and the hate.

She slid from the tree and knelt beside him. *Oh,*

Lord, she prayed silently, *show me the way to help Jordan return to You, that he might know Your love and forgiveness. And through believing in Your forgiveness of him, he might forgive himself.*

She could think of nothing appropriate to say, so taking his hand, she held it against her cheek. Abruptly, he sat up and wiped the back of his hand along her face. "You crying?" He turned her face into the moonlight and looked deep into her eyes. Then, letting go her hand, he took his handkerchief to wipe her face. "If you're weeping for me . . . don't. I'm not worth a single tear."

His voice, now sharp and brittle, cut through her, made her heart ache for him, made the tears flow hard and fast.

"Oh, yes, you are, Jordan Cooke. You're worth every one and more. And I'm sure mine aren't the first shed over you. I imagine your poor mother has cried buckets."

"Don't . . . mention my mother," he commanded, and stood suddenly, towering over her. "Get up," he demanded brusquely. "Never let me see you on your knees again."

She didn't move, but looked up into his face glowering over her. "If you were around me under normal circumstances, you'd see that I spend considerable time on them every day in prayer. I don't intend to do otherwise."

His face softened, and he extended his hand to help her stand. "No, of course you don't, and I wouldn't want it different. I just couldn't bear having you on your knees before me."

They began to walk slowly back along the road, separated from each other by the wide track. Gabrielle yearned to touch him, hold his hand, walk next to him, and bring him some comfort. But as she looked at the erect, forbidding figure staring ahead, unswerving and unbending, she lost her courage. She was strong in many ways, but if he were to reject or misunderstand her offer of companionship, she didn't think she could endure the rebuff. Not at the moment, at least. And so they returned to the hotel, each wrapped in a private agony.

Jordan lounged easily against the wall as she unlocked her door and pushed it open. She stood with her back to him, framed in the door jamb, uncertain of what to do. The emotions engendered during their talk, built on the walk back, now raged through her. Feelings for a man, her man, which she had never experienced, now attacked her as strangers with no consideration, or kindness, or gentleness. She looked down to see her hands, icy with tension, tremble as she clasped them in front of her. Tears unshed earlier forced their way to the surface and slid down her cheeks.

At last, she heard him move and then felt his arm around her, pulling her to him. Felt his face, smooth from the recent shave, as he laid his cheek against her. Smelled the warm clean scent of him, tinged with turpentine and tallow. Throbbed as he slowly turned her around to face him. Tasted the sweetness of his mouth mingled with the salt of her tears as he cradled her face in his hand and kissed her, softly, tenderly. Felt him linger on her lips, exploring them, savoring them as a butterfly does a special fragrant bud, settle back for one last sip . . . now shatter the promise, pull away, hover near. Felt their breath fuse, uniting them as one. Looked into his haunted eyes, mirroring her own hurt and longing.

He pulled her to him once more, and held her tightly with his one good arm. "Goodbye, my precious Gabby," he whispered against her cheek. "Thanks for the sweet dreams for my pillow."

He released her gently, and she searched his face one last time. Were those tears that made his eyes glisten? "Wait! Don't go," she said in hushed tones.

She let her hand slide slowly down his arm to his hand still resting on her waist, memorizing the roughness of the wool tweed of his jacket, the power of the muscles of his arm, the strength of the long supple fingers.

She moved from under his hand, warm beneath her icy touch, and hurried to her bedside. She picked up her Bible given her on her sixth birthday and the most precious thing she owned. She wanted desperately for him to have it, to make it and the memory of her a part of his life. She returned to him, clutching the worn black leather book to her breast.

"There is much comfort between these covers. Please take it." Her voice held firm, and as she extended the Bible to him, her hands ceased their trembling.

To her great joy, he took it, awkwardly held it in his right hand and opened the cover. He read the inscription and then leafed through the pages.

"It's well-used, but perhaps some of my favorite underlined verses will serve you as they have me."

Still he said nothing, only continued to riffle the pages. Then, holding the Bible in his left hand, he extended it out to her. "I can't take this. You've had it since you were a child. It has to be very dear to you."

"It is, but when I get to the ranch, I'll have Ellen's. The words are the same, you know."

She watched the slender, steel-strong fingers wrap slowly around the Bible, all the while still holding it toward her.

She gently laid her fingers over his and pressed his arm back against his chest. "Please," she pleaded and watched his chin tremble ever so slightly and the tears that had only glistened, now gathered, filling the rims of his eyes.

He folded the Bible against his heart in reverence. Then he wheeled abruptly, crossed the hall in two quick strides, and disappeared into his room.

Slowly, she closed the door to her room to form a double barrier. As she shut herself off from him, she felt the emptiness of knowing she would not see him again. Raising the window blind, she undressed by moonlight. Then, slipping between cool, crisp sheets, she sank into a freshly aired feather tick . . . all the comforts she had longed for. But instead of savoring the luxury, she lay, aware only of the image of Jordan's face the moment before he turned away, and she felt his pain sear through her.

CHAPTER 12

SUNLIGHT STREAMED THROUGH the lace-curtained window, beat on Gabrielle's bed, and flooded her room with its joy. Reluctantly she rolled over. Even through the uncomprehending haze of fatigue, she knew there was some reason she didn't want this day to begin. Slowly, in small bits, the events of last night seeped into her consciousness. Her eyes darted to the bedside stand. Yes, the Bible was gone. She hadn't dreamed those last poignant minutes. Closing her eyes, his face vivid in her mind, she could still feel the pressure of Jordan's arm across her back as he held her to him, smell the slight odor of the salve she had spread on him, taste his kiss sweet and slightly salty on her lips, and hear the terminating click of his door as it shut forever between them.

Her heart and mind resisted dealing with those final agonizing moments any longer, and so she locked last night's events away to be brought out on a day when she could fully explore and savor the nuances of each one.

Choosing a serviceable cornflower-blue calico

frock, she washed and dressed quickly in the sun-warmed room. Her traveling suit was impregnated with so much dust she disliked even having to pick it up and fold it into the travel valise with her other dirty things. She repacked her belongings and left the bags in the room while she went into the lobby to see about check-out time.

"You expectin' someone to pick you up?" the clerk asked.

She wondered if the thin little man was Mrs. Solomon's husband. "Yes. Mr. Edward Bailey is my brother-in-law, and I've come to take care of his children," she explained, hoping Mr. Bailey might have left some word for her.

"Ain't seen him yet today. Real shame about his missus. Died mighty unexpected and sudden-like. You her sister?" He said it all casually enough, but he watched her intently. Gabrielle knew that every word she uttered and every movement she made would be duly reported to all who knew the Baileys.

"Yes. Now about my luggage?"

"Kin leave it in your room as long as you want, 'lessen I need the space. Not likely, though. Don't rent that room real often. Best room in the house. Costs too much for most folks. 'Cept that Mr. Cooke. He don't seem to pay no never mind to how much he spends for anythin'. Real nice man, him. Real nice."

The emotions of last night were still too new and close to the surface for Gabrielle to control well. She didn't want to discuss Jordan this morning. "Thank you. I shall be in the dining room in case Mr. Bailey should arrive."

"I'll tell him." But with the tenacity of a born gossip, he intuitively knew her sensitive area and pursued it with the perseverance of a hound dog. "Mr. Cooke rode out real early this morning. Didn't look like he'd slept much. Looked hung-over, bad."

Gabrielle's breath quickened at the mention of

Jordan's condition, and her heart did little out-of-rhythm skips. She wondered if his arm hurt, wanted desperately to see if it was all right, and put some more salve on it. *Gabrielle, you aren't going to see him again, ever. Now start thinking about Mr. Bailey and the children.*

"Thank you," she repeated, and hurried into the dining room before the eager prattler noticed something in her behavior he could report to the Basin folks.

She helped herself to a steaming mug of coffee from the pitcher on the sideboard. That was all she wanted. She chose a seat by a window that looked out on the road just in case Mr. Bailey should drive up. As she finished her coffee, from somewhere inside the hotel, she heard a clock strike ten. It was early yet. Probably too early for him to finish the chores and get to town.

She couldn't sit any more, and she felt she had time for a walk. The town crier at the hotel desk would be sure Mr. Bailey knew her whereabouts should he arrive before she returned. Secure in this knowledge, she set out for a brisk hike. She wondered which way Jordan had ridden. *Now, Gabrielle, you may not think more about him today. You have other things with which to occupy your mind.* Her lecture was delivered in the stern no-nonsense manner she used on uncooperative patients. However, it was difficult to think about Mr. Bailey and the children because she only had Ellen's descriptions to go by. She had never seen photographs of the family.

She walked briskly, felt the spring sun beat on her back, and watched it draw life back into the high mountain valley after the lifelessness of winter. It revelled in the fields of wildflowers, blending their colors like those on a painter's pallet. The breeze, heavy laden with the fragrance of May lilacs, cooled her, and when she grew thirsty, she stopped at the tumbling stream, parted the watercress, and scooped

153

up handfuls of icy cold water, fresh from large snow fields in the nearby high mountains. Then she knelt at the stream's edge and said her morning prayers, thanked the Lord for His goodness and mercy, for setting her heart free from the bonds of the deep hatred she had held there so long. She thanked Him for bringing her so far, safely, and thanked Him for Jordan and the kindness he had shown her. She asked for protection for Jordan as he traveled, prayed for the Lord to find room in Jordan's heart, to bring him peace and self-forgiveness. Gabrielle meditated for a time beside the stream, letting the peace of the valley fill her and give her strength to face her unknown future.

When she returned to the hotel, she felt refreshed and comforted. It was only later as she sat in the lobby reading, that it occurred to her she hadn't mentioned the Baileys once in her prayers. She quickly bowed her head and corrected the omission.

Listening to the clock strike twelve sent little sparks of concern through Gabrielle. Soon, she was going to have to think about a course of action if Mr. Bailey didn't come. She didn't want to even think how much the room cost, but the thought of sleeping in accommodations less comfortable and clean wasn't appealing, either.

"Ma'am," the clerk called across the lobby.

Gabrielle hurried to the counter. "Yes? Have you word of Mr. Bailey?"

"'Fraid not. Just wanted to tell you not to fret none if Bailey don't get here. Mr. Cooke told me to see you had your room long as you needed it. Paid for it for a week and said he'd be back then. If you was still here, said he'd take care of everything."

Her temper flashed. "He can't do that. I'm no charity case."

"He said you'd probably act up a bit, but I was to ignore you. Said your manners wasn't very good. Said you kicked like a mule."

She made her hand into a fist and whacked the counter. "Oh, he did, did he!" she sputtered, before turning on her heel and storming outside. Once outside, however, she couldn't help laughing. *Kicked like a mule.* He wasn't going to let her forget her breach of conduct, even when he wasn't around to remind her.

She looked up and down the road, but there saw no tell-tale trail of dust to indicate any traffic. Since she had had no breakfast, she decided to eat lunch. If the Baileys hadn't eaten before they arrived, she could join them and have a cup of coffee.

As she started through the lobby toward the dining room, the ever observant little man motioned her over to the desk. "Mr. Cooke also paid for your meals, so don't be shy. Eat what you like. Maude's a great cook."

Gabrielle nodded her thanks, but inside she wanted to scream at Jordan to stop tearing her heart with his thoughtfulness when she would never see him again to thank him, or to perform a reciprocating act. Pain stabbed through her, knowing these were the last caring things he would ever do for her. She wanted to be angry with him for his intrusion in her life. Anger she could deal with. This rending emotional ache where her heart should be, left her helpless.

She vowed not to take advantage of his generosity beyond today and to think no more on him. Some day, a long time from now, when the love she bore him had dimmed, when she was happily married and he no longer mattered so desperately, she would let the past three days surface and wonder what had happened to him. Some day, a very, very long time from now.

Commanding the tears to stay behind her eyelids and willing her chin to stop trembling, she quickly found herself an inconspicuous corner table in the nearly empty room. A couple of cowhands had wandered in a bit earlier, but they sat in the far end of the room. A girl, unknown to Gabrielle, served her a delicious-looking casserole and cottage cheese and fruit. What a wonderful change from the meat, potatoes, and greasy gravy she had tried to subsist on the past few days. If the lump in her throat would move over, maybe she could swallow some of the lunch.

It was one o'clock when she finished eating. Now she began to feel pangs of real concern. Perhaps one of the family was ill. With children that small, it would be impossible to leave a sick child alone, and Ellen had written they had no close neighbors. And of course, if Mr. Bailey were ill, the children were too little to hitch a team and drive to town. When her vivid imagination started to work, she found it impossible to sit still, and so she went out on the porch where she could see the road, and paced away an hour.

Two o'clock. The sun, now westerly, shone onto the hotel porch. It began getting warm, and even dressed in calico, Gabrielle could feel perspiration forming along her backbone. She was just ready to give up and seek the cool of the inside when she spied a trail of dust coming down a lesser used road from the mountain.

She shielded her eyes and stood, watching the distant speck turn into a wagon. It finally drew close enough so she could see a splendidly dressed man driving the team. She ran a nervous hand over the coil of hair at the nape of her neck and dabbed her face and neck with her handkerchief. It certainly wouldn't do to let Mr. Bailey see her perspiring like a field hand. She smoothed her bodice, her waist, and tugged at the skirt to straighten it.

When the unpainted, weathered buckboard pulled to a stop in front of the hotel steps, she could hardly contain herself. Licking her lips and remembering not to smile too widely, she said, "Mr. Edward Bailey?"

A perfectly groomed, well-built man dressed in an impeccably tailored suit of the latest design stepped down from the dilapidated old wagon. The contrast jarred Gabrielle for a moment, and then she forgot as he bowed, "Miss Gabrielle Sevier?"

"Why, yes," she stammered and extended her hand.

He brushed a kiss across it with just the right touch. "I do hope we haven't kept you waiting too long. One of my team developed a problem in the night, and we were unable to travel as rapidly as I would have liked."

Gabrielle looked at the poor, bony animal leaning in the traces. *That problem didn't develop in the night*, she thought. *It's been about twenty years in the making*. But she had the good manners to keep her thoughts to herself.

A timid little voice issued from the wagon box. "Can we sit up yet, Papa?"

"Oh," he acted startled, like he had forgotten the little girls were there. "Why, yes."

Two little faces, washed clean, peered over the edge of the wagon. Their unwashed light brown hair, however, was matted, the tangles scarcely disturbed by a poor attempt at combing. Amy raised a grubby hand and absent-mindedly scratched a healing scab on her arm. Sarah, brown eyes wide in a too-thin face, wiped her badly running nose with the back of her hand. They stood, revealing unironed tattered dresses: too small on Sarah; too large on Amy.

Mr. Bailey turned but appeared to look past the girls. "Say hello to your Aunt Gabrielle and give her a big hug," he instructed.

Gabrielle stood distressed, looking from children to father. The contrast was striking. She fixed a weak smile before moving toward the wagon to be welcomed by her little nieces. They shrank from her reaching arms, though, and huddled together like two little animals, distrust filling their eyes.

"Girls had a few problems since Ellen died. They'll be fine, now you're here. Taking care of children is woman's work and a man just can't do it right. You're sorely needed. Mighty grateful to you for coming."

Unable to think of anything polite to say, she nodded her answer. However, she fully agreed with him. Her decision to come had been right—or at least it would be. Thank heaven, she could put things right with a healthy application of soap and water. She fairly itched to get started.

"Have you eaten?" she asked.

"Had a sandwich on the way," he said, but two little heads shook no behind him as he spoke.

Had he actually eaten in front of the children and not fed them, or was he putting on a front? Gabrielle didn't know which to think, but she wasn't taking any chances. "The clerk at the desk can show you where my luggage is. If you will load it, I'll ask Mrs. Solomon to pack us a picnic. We'll be able to eat on the way to the ranch and not have to fret about preparing a meal when we get there this evening."

He opened his mouth, but she turned and hurried away before he could say anything. Her mind raced as she gave Mrs. Solomon instructions for the picnic basket. What kind of man was he? Handsome, mannerly, a real dandy from the way he dressed. But there was something wrong if he would work a tired old horse behind a wagon, and allow children to go dirty and hungry. *Now, Gabrielle, you're jumping to conclusions. You've known the man fewer than ten minutes. There are probably good explanations for everything.*

Carrying the basket filled with food, she stopped by her room for her cape and purse. Returning to the wagon, she noticed the two horses standing unmoved. "Have you watered your animals and given them some food?"

A look of helpless indecision settled on his face.

"Well, actually, no. We're so late, I hated to take the time. I think they'll be all right until we get home." He smiled a pathetic little smile at her.

Gabrielle didn't like the way he passed off the normal attention anyone would pay their animals, especially if they had to travel any distance. "Just how far is home?"

"About ten miles."

"Up that mountain?"

His eyes lowered and he bowed his head. "Not all the way up," he answered in a thin voice.

Although feeling she treaded perilously close to the limit of her bounds and might incur his anger, she refused to allow him to exert the team further without supplying them with food and water first. "Even so, I will not proceed until these beasts have been cared for. If money is a problem, I have some. I shall pay for the livery service. Drive them there now, please." She stormed around the wagon and climbed unassisted into the high seat.

He mounted his side and after considerable urging, finally managed to get the team to move to the livery stable where they were fed and watered.

"Please include a large sack of oats in the bill and a spare bucket if you have one so that we may feed them later," she directed. Doubts about Mr. Bailey and his ability to provide grew by the minute.

At last, she was satisfied with the preparations, and they began the return trip. If her calculations were correct, they should arrive home about six o'clock. . .well before dark.

The girls curled up on a musty, smelly quilt in the back, still unwilling to give or accept any overtures of friendship. That was all right. Gabrielle had worked with enough children to know that if they weren't forced and when they had had time to get used to her, things would be fine. She could wait, especially until she had a chance to bathe them.

The road was little used and rough. She had thought the rocking of the stagecoach difficult, but this was by far the worst beating she had ever taken. It became impossible to talk, for the bouncing and pounding over the rocks and through the holes literally jounced the air from their lungs. They had been traveling for about an hour when she noticed the road ahead turn sharply and disappear up the mountain.

"Does the road get steep at this point?" she asked.

"Some," he answered briefly.

Now she realized the road wasn't the only reason they had been riding in silence. He was still angry at her for telling him what to do. Well, that was too bad. If he didn't know to do what was right, then he would have to put up with her telling him. . .like now.

"There's a nice stream to water the horses and a good place to pull off. We can have our picnic while the team rests and eats a bit. Then, we'll all be refreshed and ready to climb the hill."

She watched the muscles set granite-like in his jaw, and she thought for a minute he planned to proceed on without regard for her suggestion. However, at the last possible second, he pulled the wagon off the road and to the bank of the stream. While he unhitched the team, Gabrielle spread the lunch. Then she walked over and leaned into the wagon box.

"Would you girls let me help you down? You can wash and then we'll eat. Mrs. Solomon has prepared a very special treat for you."

The girls crawled along the quilt to the end of the wagon where they permitted Gabrielle to lift them to the ground. She was used to lifting children and couldn't believe how little these girls weighed. Under their ill-fitting clothes, they must be skin and bones.

Without soap and warm water, hardly anything could be accomplished against the ground-in grime on their hands, but Gabrielle removed a couple of layers in the little brook.

Mr. Bailey finished tending to the team and joined them. The children sat contentedly on the ground, Mr. Bailey found a fallen log, and Gabrielle perched primly on a large flat rock.

She assumed the role of hostess, a long-time dream fulfilled. "Would you bless the food, please, Mr. Bailey."

He nodded his consent and gave brief thanks. Gabrielle served the lunch, delicious roast beef sandwiches, homemade mustard pickles, carrot strips, and big oatmeal cookies filled with raisins. The children began eating like they were starved, and Mr. Bailey continually scolded them for their manners. They tried to do as he wished, but it seemed impossible for them to please him. Gabrielle's heart ached for the little girls, but she refrained from speaking. She had angered their father enough for one day. When they had settled into a routine and gotten to know one another, then she would teach them manners in private.

The children finished and scurried to the stream for a drink and to toss pebbles into the water. Gabrielle was left alone with Mr. Bailey for the first time.

"You certainly live out in the country," she commented.

"Didn't always live so far. When Ellen was here, we had a ranch out the other way from Marsh Basin. Had a nice house and she kept things up real well." A lonesome wistful look made his pretty but weak-looking face even less forceful.

"Why did you move?"

"Just couldn't stand it there without her. I tried to sell, but buyers aren't standing in line when there's so much land that's free. She managed the money and everything. When she went, things sort of fell apart. I went prospecting and found some abandoned claims and an old cabin. It was too far to travel back and forth, and I couldn't leave the girls alone that much, so we moved up here last spring."

His voice had a powerless whine to it, and Gabrielle found it extremely irritating, particularly after Jordan's deep resonant voice that rolled with strength, except when he was in pain.

"I'm not much of a manager. Ellen did so much. . ." His voice trailed off and he sat, head bowed.

This wasn't the strong-sounding gentleman of the letters. What had happened to change him? Had he been this way when Ellen married him? Surely not. No sane woman would consider marriage to the likes of him. But then Ellen didn't know him except as Gabrielle did, through his letters. However, they hadn't married immediately. He must be too deep in his grief to function normally. Gabrielle tried desperately to sort out her findings.

The trip up the mountain was a nightmare Gabrielle would not soon forget. What kept the old horse from dropping dead in the traces, she didn't know. It not only hadn't the strength to pull its share of the load, it laid back against the traces, and that made a terrible burden for the beautiful young stallion. Finally, after a last dreadful grade when Mr. Bailey brought out a whip and laid it over the back of the old horse, the pair pulled the wagon up in front of a small log cabin built with a sod roof and its back against the mountain.

Gabrielle jumped down and helped the children out. Carrying two of her bags, she followed the silent girls into the house. While the light only filtered through one incredibly dirty window, there was enough to see the unbelievable disorder. This obviously had not been Ellen's home. She would never have lived like this, nor permitted her family to do so. Mr. Bailey hadn't even brought the furniture from their other house. This place was furnished with crude handmade furniture, unskilled hands had built the cabin, and it had a dirt floor covered with rubble. Gabrielle stood gaping, too stunned to move further into the room.

A little jerk on her skirt returned her to mobility. "Yes," she said and looked down into Sarah's upturned face.

"Amy's foot's bleedin' again," she said in a tiny, frightened voice.

Gabrielle looked to see blood seeping between the toes of the little foot. Looked closer and noticed both girls had a multitude of wounds in various stages of healing. Clearing a spot on the dish-filled table, she sat Amy up and inspected the cut. It was infected and would need attention.

Reluctantly, she placed her bags down on the floor next to the bedroom door. Her mind leaped ahead, organizing a plan of action. When she got a fire started, she could heat some water and bathe the children. Then, using the remedies she had brought, she could treat and bandage Amy's foot. If she stayed off it for a few days, it would heal and all would be well.

This was a fine plan, but when she went for wood, the woodbox was empty. She could find nothing to burn anywhere around. Mr. Bailey entered as she finished making her survey.

"I don't seem to find any wood to start a fire," she said.

"I'm afraid there isn't any. I used the last of it to heat water this morning," he whined in a pitiful voice. But he made no offer to find more.

Gabrielle decided there was no need for diplomacy. This useless man needed a stick of dynamite under him. Pulling herself up to her full height, she placed her hands on her hips and glared at him, eye to eye.

"Then I suggest you change your clothes and go out to get some. Amy's foot is infected and I must heat water in order to treat her. Besides, both children badly need baths."

He collapsed into a chair and held his head in his hands. "I've had a terrible day. The feisty horse got

163

away from me this morning and I had to chase him over half the mountain. Then I had to chop wood for heating water. Girls wouldn't get into the tub when I'd finished bathing. I was lucky to get their faces washed, way they acted. I try to keep their cuts clean, but they just seem to delight in scratching themselves up. When I work in the mine all day, I can't be expected to come back and cook and clean and all those things.''

Gabrielle began to wonder if his tirade would ever end.

''I'm afraid if you want hot water, you'll have to cut your own wood. I'm just too tired to do it tonight. I must go and lie down or I shall surely have an attack.'' He hobbled into the bedroom like an old man, and she could hear the latch as he set it on the crudely made slab door.

Gabrielle tried to convince herself she was imagining all this. It really wasn't happening. However, dreaming or not, she found an ax and taking the children with her lest they start playing and disturb their father, trudged out to find firewood. Before it grew too dark to see, she cut enough wood to make a fire and keep it burning for awhile.

Maintaining a cheerful voice for the sake of the children, Gabrielle chatted with the girls as she set a pot of water on the stove. ''I'm sorry there won't be time to heat enough water for baths tonight, but I will take care of your foot, Amy. Then, tomorrow, we'll get a big stack of wood and make enough hot water to really clean this place up. How does that sound?''

She was finally rewarded with a timid little smile from the shy child clinging to Sarah's hand.

''Amy thinks that's just fine,'' Sarah translated.

''Doesn't Amy talk?'' Gabrielle asked as she busied herself stacking the dishes and trying to make enough room to move.

''Sometimes, but she's scared most of the time and so she doesn't.''

"What's she scared of?"

"Papa, when he gets mad. He gets real mad at us."

Gabrielle had to fight tears. These poor little dears, abused by that horrible man in the next room. She didn't know what she was going to do, but tomorrow she would have to make some serious decisions.

Amy's foot was finally bandaged and a few layers of dirt removed from each little girl. Gabrielle tucked them into their bunks, found some spare quilts in a trunk, and spread them on the floor for herself. Evening prayers were brief before exhaustion obliterated the dreadful situation.

Although the grime on the window dimmed the sun, it still succeeded in pouring through the wretched cabin. When the beam hit Gabrielle's face, she jerked her eyes open and found herself staring along the dirt floor piled with empty tin cans, stacks of dirty clothes, old newspapers and more. She felt like she had slept the night at the garbage dump. It smelled like she had. What would these two girls have done if she hadn't arrived? She thanked God He had brought her.

Curious, though. Why did Mr. Bailey take such care for her welfare, making sure she had the best accommodations? Was he afraid she wouldn't come? Because he knew the conditions, did he feel somehow the knowledge of them might be transmitted to her? She let a myriad of questions and thoughts ramble as she dressed in the cold room.

The children didn't stir even as she built a fire, and there was no sound from behind the closed bedroom door. The lazy creature would probably snore until noon, Gabrielle fumed silently. When the fire was going well, she found the bucket and opened the door to go in search of fresh water.

There, on the door at eye level, she saw an envelope stuck into a cross brace. She removed it, set the bucket down, and tore out the letter inside. Familiar handwriting leaped off the page at her.

To Miss Gabrielle Sevier: Being of sound mind and body, I hearby give her all my claim to the cabin and the acre of ground it sits on, the mining claims and full custody of her sister's children, Sarah and Amy. She is henceforth from today responsible for any debts I may have accrued and entitled to any profits I may have earned.

I'm not a fit parent for these children and without Ellen I just can't manage. I do hope you'll all find it in your heart to forgive me one day.

(signed) Edward Bailey

Gabrielle read it twice to be sure she wasn't dreaming. Dashing across the debris-strewn floor, she flung open the bedroom door. The bedclothes were thrown back and the room was empty. She examined the clothes cupboard. Ellen's clothes were still hanging there, but there were no man's belongings. Rushing back outside, she found the wagon standing where they had stopped last night. At least, she had transportation. *The horses!* Running down the incline to the rude shelter, she found the pitiful, broken-down old dapple scarcely able to stand. The beautiful stallion was gone and Mr. Bailey had taken part of the oats she had bought.

What a disappointment Ellen's husband had turned out to be. And Gabrielle cringed when she thought that she had allowed herself to even dream that they might marry. Since he obviously cared for no one but himself, he would probably never marry again. At least, not to the likes of her, she decided.

She needed to hear her voice and so she talked to the only thing around. "Well, old horse, what are we going to do now?"

He looked at her with woeful eyes and gave a low nicker. "I couldn't agree more. It's a mess, but strangely I feel much better with that spineless, whimpering man gone. With the Lord's help, we'll make it."

The horse shook his head vigorously. "Yes, you'll make it too. We're not leaving here without you."

CHAPTER 13

GABRIELLE COULDN'T BELIEVE a month had passed. She had been so busy setting up housekeeping, the time fairly flew. Although still a crude cabin, it was now clean and livable. She had moved the girls' rudely made bunk beds into the bedroom and arranged it so the three of them could sleep comfortably. The other room thus became their commons area.

She had found garden seeds sent to Ellen last spring and left unplanted. With a bit of searching, she located a small patch of sunny fertile ground and had dug the virgin soil to plant a garden. Lettuce and radishes would soon be big enough to eat. Beets and chard were doing well, and the peas and beans looked healthy. She could hardly wait for the fresh things to be ready. In Nashville, gardens were already producing, and she hungered for the fresh vegetables she had left.

Her biggest worry had been milk for the children. However, she discovered some cases of canned milk and by adding a bit of chocolate and sugar, flavored it so they drank willingly.

167

No great seamstress like her sister, she could, nevertheless, sew a bit. Gabrielle had cut Ellen's things down into proper-sized dresses and underwear for the girls. Now, she sat outside in the warmth of the afternoon sun watching her two nieces, sparkling clean and healthy, happily playing house under the wagon. Her hands never still, she stitched small summer nightgowns made from Ellen's own.

What worried her most was what they were going to do come winter. They couldn't stay here, and yet they hadn't been visited by a single soul from whom they might seek help. They just might have to walk out, buy a suitable team, and ride them back to get the wagon and their things. Thank God for Jordan and the money he had paid her.

If she had a good team, they could perhaps travel west to Boise, and she could get work as a nurse. Better, they might go north to Butte in the Montana Territory. There were lots of medical problems around mines, and the eastern attitude toward nurses didn't seem to hold here in the West. She had been treated with respect and accorded admiration and esteem. . .very different from being classed as a prostitute or a servant.

Hoofbeats along the road broke into her thoughts. *Good heavens, company!* She smoothed her hair and set aside her sewing. "Come girls, let's welcome whoever is arriving to see us."

The children left their play and stood, folded into her skirts, as a large, rough-looking man rode into the yard. "You Mrs. Bailey?" he asked, still mounted and giving no introduction.

"Who wants to know?" Gabrielle asked in return. Who did he think he was?

"Ain't got time for guessin' games. Where's Bailey?"

His voice, gravelly and harsh, frightened the children, and they each grabbed one of her legs through her skirts and clung tenaciously. "I don't know."

168

"Said he was leavin' and you was responsible for his debts. Said you had money." He thrust a piece of paper out to her.

She unlatched the girls enough to walk toward him as he rode up and handed her the paper. It was a note signed by Edward Bailey for two hundred dollars and dated a week before he had sent her the train ticket. So that was where the horse, new clothes, and her transportation had come from.

"I don't have this kind of money," she said. "I can't possibly pay it."

He scanned the poor place. "Not much here. He leave you the minin' claims, too?"

"That, sir, is none of your business," she snapped.

"Ma'am, until I get my money, all your property is my business. I don't take kindly to people runnin' out on their rightful owed debts." He turned a savage look on her.

The man unnerved her, but she refused to let him know how frightened she was. She kept her voice steady and her chin tilted in defiance. "And what if I can't pay? Are you going to have two helpless children and a woman thrown in jail?"

His eyes narrowed and he ran them over her body, leaving her no doubts about what he would do to her. She felt scalded by his appraisal, terrified at its implications.

"I'll be back in two weeks. Don't try to pack up and leave, either. I always get what's owed me . . . one way or t'other." He spat a stream of tobacco juice which landed just short of her shoe, turned his horse, and rode out of sight into the trees.

She prayed the children wouldn't feel her trembling as they clutched each other and Sarah clung to Gabrielle's hand. She must keep calm.

Desperate, she knelt so she was eye-level with the girls. "Remember, children, we are never alone. God is always watching over us—even when we sleep.

And sometimes He sends His helpers, too. Why, I think I met one of them on my trip!'' And before she knew it, she had made up a tale of a delightful mountain man, 'Mr. McKim,' praying fervently for forgiveness all the while. ''Mr. McKim lives somewhere around these parts and is very likely trapping right here in these mountains. He could drop in to see us any day. That dreadful man wouldn't stand a chance against Mr. McKim.''

It was a pitiful ruse, but it worked. Sarah smiled and gave an exaggerated sigh of relief and Amy imitated her. ''We'll just look for Mr. McKim. How will we know him?''

Gabrielle led the children to the porch and described in detail the imaginary Mr. McKim. Indeed, the description was so vivid and came so quickly to mind that she felt strangely inspired and comforted at the same time. Perhaps she had merely named the guardian angel that surely hovered just out of human view. At least the girls were growing more hopeful by the moment. She enjoyed the telling as much as they did, and by the time she was finished had almost convinced herself of the possibility of his appearance.

She was able to keep up a confident front until evening, but as soon as the girls were asleep, she took Ellen's Bible and went out on the porch to seek comfort and help. It was still light enough in the afterglow to read, but this Bible wasn't marked, and she did miss hers. Knowing Jordan was reading it, however, gave her solace, and made the giving worth the sacrifice. She opened the book and let her eyes rest on the last verses of Psalm 145.

She read aloud, ''The Lord is nigh unto all them that call upon him, to all that call upon him in truth. He will fulfil the desire of them that fear him: he also will hear their cry and will save them.'' Closing the Bible, she prayed, ''Oh Lord, thank You. I shall carry these words in my heart and shall speak Your praise, knowing that we shall be saved from harm." Calmed by the promise, she carried the message to bed and slept soundly.

In the morning before the girls awakened, she took her purse from the chest in the bedroom and laid out her money on the kitchen table. She counted it several times, but, due to her shopping spree in Salt Lake City and the expense of the livery care for the team, she was seven dollars short of the sum the man had demanded. And if she did pay all her money, then how would she buy a team? They couldn't live here in the winter. Sarah had told of the snow covering the window and drifting across the door after they had come in the spring. It had taken her father all day to shovel them clear. And Gabrielle knew she couldn't cut enough wood to last a month, much less five or six. No, they could not stay here, and if she attempted to pay the debt, they would have no way of leaving.

Slipping to her knees on the newly braided rug now covering the dirt floor under the table, she prayed. "I know you gave me the promise yesterday that You would preserve those who love You. Lord, I'm holding You to that. You are our only salvation. Without You, we can do nothing. But just remember, Lord, he's giving You only two weeks. Amen."

There was no calendar, but Gabrielle had carved a notch on a long stick for each day since she had arrived. Now, she went out and marked a line before she cut the notch for today. She wanted to make sure she kept accurate count of these next two weeks. *Rather like keeping track of the arrival of doomsday*, she thought dismally. *Gabrielle, you promised the Lord you'd praise Him and let Him solve your problem. Now, do it!*

Straightening her shoulders and setting her chin, she marched into the house and wakened the children. "Good morning, ladies. Rise and shine." She sat down on the edge of the lower bunk where Amy stretched and, still rosy with sleep, held up her arms for the hug to which she had become accustomed.

Sarah, clutching the elegant doll Gabrielle had brought her, leaned over to receive her hug and let Gabrielle lift her down.

"We're going to have to build a ladder so you can get in and out by yourself. But we won't do that today. Today, we're going exploring. We've worked so hard, we haven't taken time to see what's around us. Would you like that?"

"Oh, yes, Aunt Gabrielle!" Sarah danced around in little circles with Amy tagging behind in her version of the celebration. "Where are we goin'? Are we goin' to take a picnic? You've been promisin' us a picnic for days." Sarah chattered non-stop as she dressed herself, and then set her beautiful doll on Gabrielle's bed. She didn't show up enough on the bunk, Sarah said. Down on the big bed, she could see her often and talk to Miss DeWitt when she needed to. Sarah had chosen that name for the doll after Gabrielle described the glamorous Melanie.

With the lunches packed, they started out along the wagon road which went on up the mountain. Gabrielle had restrained her curiosity while she put their lives in order. But since the days now seemed to be numbered, it gave her the excuse she needed to break free for a day. They climbed slowly along the sun-patched road, little-used and over-grown with grasses and weeds.

"Where are we goin'?" Sarah asked.

"I haven't any idea. We'll just walk and be surprised by what we find."

Sarah and Amy chased dancing butterflies, picked brilliant wildflowers, and ran, happy and laughing, ahead and brought back their wondrous discoveries to show Gabrielle. Her heart swelled at the sight and sound of the beautiful little girls, growing strong and joyous under her loving care. In her eyes, at least, they were beautiful. Amy truly was. She had soft blond curls, wide china-blue eyes, and a shy bow-shaped smile. Sarah's beauty, however, would have to come from inside, for, as Ellen had written, the child looked like a miniature Gabrielle. For this, and in spite of her better judgment, Gabrielle loved Sarah best.

The little-used wagon trail they walked along joined a well-used road about a mile above their cabin. Recently, heavily loaded wagons pulled by well-shod draft horses had passed long the route. Gabrielle wondered why she hadn't heard the sounds, then realized the constant wind through the evergreen trees and the never-ceasing babble of the stream near the house would have drowned out the sound.

"Let's walk along this road. The people who've travelled it recently might still be on the mountain," Gabrielle suggested.

"Mr. McKim might be up there, too," Sarah said, and grabbed Amy's hand to pull her along faster.

This caused the little one to balk. "I's tired. I's not walkin' any more." To prove her point, she plunked her body firmly on a small rock and refused to budge. No amount of coaxing from Sarah and Gabrielle would convince her to move.

"I wonder if Amy is so hungry she can't go farther," Gabrielle said.

A vigorous nod of the little head proved Gabrielle right.

"Very well. This is a fine place to eat. We'll rest and have our lunch. Then, Amy will be strong and can walk up the mountain." Gabrielle unpacked the food, and they all ate heartily the sandwiches of homemade bread, canned meat, and watercress. After a cool drink from one of the many springs dotting the mountain, Gabrielle handed out oatmeal cookies for dessert.

Now, having eaten her fill, Amy wanted to curl up for a nap. Walking further up the mountain seemed something she would postpone forever. Gabrielle sighed, hiding her disappointment, and pulled Amy onto her lap.

"If I promise not to go far, could I walk up the road? Maybe somebody's there and knows about Mr. McKim," Sarah appealed.

Gabrielle understood curiosity and knew Sarah would keep her word about not going far. "Yes, Sarah. But the first time you get tired and need to rest will be the sign you are to turn around and come back."

"All right. And I'll tell you all I see," she promised before disappearing behind the sharp turn around a rock outcropping.

Gabrielle sat with her back against a tree, holding the sleeping child. The droning bees and visiting flies created a lazy hum which relaxed her and she, too, dozed.

"Aunt Gabrielle, Aunt Gabrielle," Sarah's musical voice sang through the forest.

Gabrielle roused and called, "Right over here, Sarah."

Sarah came skipping down the road, and threw herself down next to Gabrielle. Amy stirred and stretched, opened a sleepy eye and blinked several times before deciding it was all right to open the other.

"I saw four empty wagons and lots of big, big horses," Sarah bubbled. "I could hear men's voices coming out of a hole in the mountain, but I couldn't see anyone. I'm sure Mr. McKim was there. I could hear him. He has a big deep voice. I stayed in the trees, because the horses were everywhere and I was scared of them." She stopped and looked at Gabrielle for approval.

"You did wonderfully well. Now, in case we should need help, we know there are people working in a mine not too far from our house. That is a great comfort, for they surely would take us down the mountain if we asked."

"Shall I go back and ask?" Sarah volunteered eagerly.

"No, not today. We aren't ready to leave the mountain. If you're not too tired, though, we should start for home."

"I want to go home," Amy said. "I's not tired now."

They walked slowly down the hill, holding hands, and singing the hymns and children's songs Gabrielle had been teaching them. As they turned off the road, Gabrielle noticed a rather distinct path she had missed on the way up. "I would like to explore this trail just a minute. Can you girls stay here and wait?"

"We'll stay right here and I'll play with Amy," Sarah promised.

"I'll only be a few minutes," Gabrielle said and gathered up her skirts so she could walk faster. The trail was narrow and seemed to wind along the face of the mountain, but she couldn't see out because of the trees and undergrowth. It ended with startling abruptness at an opening into the mountain, and down the hill was a large pile of dirt and rocks, obviously dug from the hole.

Standing on the edge of the small clearing, she could look down on the sod roof of the cabin. "Is this the mine claim he left me?" she wondered aloud. Since it was so close, it must be, she decided. Hurrying back, she found Sarah entertaining Amy with a story about Mr. McKim coming to rescue them. That dear man had become a folk hero in his own time and most likely would never know about it.

By the time they arrived home, deep shadows covered the clearing by the cabin. Gabrielle hurried to feed the horse, and Sarah filled the bucket at the stream, then waited for Gabrielle to come carry it.

Amy played contentedly on the front porch with a cloth-stuffed ball Gabrielle had made her, batting it with a smooth stick.

The few chores attended to, Gabrielle and the children went inside where she built a fire to take the chill of the evening from the cabin and to heat water for sponge baths. And so, she thought, ends the first day. Thirteen more to go.

CHAPTER 14

THE NUMBERED DAYS PASSED. busy and prayerful. Gabrielle refused to think beyond, but tried to fill each day with happiness and lovely memories for the children. The three of them lived, sheltered by the mountain, safe and secure from harm. She had never felt more contented, her major struggle being to keep thoughts of Jordan from intruding. However, the morning of the fourteenth day, she awoke tense and even after prayers had difficulty maintaining her calm. The lust-filled eyes of that horrid man seemed everywhere she turned.

She thought about taking food and hiding in the mine shaft, but that would only postpone the inevitable. He would not be put off that easily, especially for so large a sum as she owed him. No, she decided, it was best to face the crisis when it came and have done with it, whatever the outcome. Today, they would follow what had become their routine . . . feed the old horse, carry and heat water and tidy the cabin, cut wood and tend the garden.

The day began cloudy and grew sultry. When the

heat of the mid-July afternoon became oppressive, they gathered quilts and took refuge in a shady nook by the stream near the cabin. There in the cool, the children napped, and Gabrielle read.

Sarah woke first. "Did Mr. McKim come?" she asked, stretching and rubbing the sleep from her eyes.

Gabrielle closed her book, the essays by Emerson she had bought as a gift to Mr. Bailey. "No. Why do you ask?"

"Because I dreamed a man came riding up. He had the money to save us," she answered. "Only he didn't look like you said Mr. McKim did. He was a big man with light hair and no beard." She stared woefully into the creek. "I sure wish he'd hurry, but I guess he's comin' as fast as he can."

Why would Sarah describe Jordan? She knew nothing of him. Gabrielle had never mentioned anything beyond the fact she had nursed a man on the train. To hide her confusion and yearning, she smiled and made her voice teasing. "You've never seen such a man as you told me about, have you?"

Sarah nodded, responding seriously to Gabrielle's question. "Once. I was hidin' up by the road. He rode down the trail to the mine. Then he left. He didn't see me."

It wasn't possible. Jordan's claims were on the Snake River. He had told her that when he told her about the dredge. *Oh, Sarah dear, I wish you hadn't brought up this subject.*

Amy woke and Gabrielle entertained them with stories, helped Sarah study her reading lesson from the Bible, and then, together, they harvested vegetables from the garden for their evening meal. They felt a cool breeze as they came up the hill and into the clearing in front of the cabin, hands full of fresh produce. Flicks of sheet lightning played across the dark gray clouds.

Sarah stopped and cocked her head. "I hear someone coming," she whispered.

Gabrielle listened, but it was impossible to hear anything over the pounding of her heart. Clearing her throat, she said, "Then we best put our greens on the porch and greet our guest," amazed at how normal she sounded. *Lord, give me strength to face the coming ordeal. Please protect these innocent children . . .*

Her prayer was cut short as their visitor rode out of the woods. He maintained a poker face when he saw them. But a noticeable pallor, accented by the royal blue of his shirt, spread over his face to give hint of the emotions lurking beneath.

"What are you doing here?" Jordan asked, his deep rolling voice betraying nothing. His shoulder now healed, he swung easily out of the saddle, untied the familiar portfolio, and walked in sure strides toward Gabrielle, his long firm legs richly booted in calf-high leather.

Sarah tugged on Gabrielle's yellow calico skirt. "That's the man I saw," she whispered.

Gabrielle nodded through tears of joy at seeing him. She was anguished that he should find her in these circumstances, and she resisted her towering love for him. These all conspired to take her voice.

He stopped a short distance away, removed his wide-brimmed Stetson, and she could see his eyes, deep jade green, begin to twinkle. "Enjoy this moment, girls," he said lightly, and gave the children a wide friendly smile. "You'll probably never again see your Aunt Gabby speechless." He turned teasing eyes on Gabrielle, and she looked to see golden flecks swimming in their depths.

Still, Gabrielle stood silent, rooted to the spot. Amy slipped a timid hand inside Gabrielle's and huddled close.

Suddenly, Jordan became all business. "Do you know an Edmund Hailey?" he asked in a crisp voice. "He owns three mining claims in this area, and I want

179

to buy them. Need them to prevent any problems that might interfere with my mine development up on the hill.'' He opened the portfolio and took out papers showing proof of the ownership.

At last Gabrielle found her voice. ''That's your mine shaft? I thought you had a dredge on the river.''

''I do, but Idaho doesn't limit a man to one kind of mining. This hard rock mine's beginning to pay rather well, and I want to expand. These claims are in the way.''

''Have you searched all the claims in the area?''

''I have and these are the only ones.'' He offered them to Gabrielle to read.

''None for an Edward Bailey?''

''None, else I would have suspected you were here.''

So that's why Mr. Bailey had so generously left her the mining claims. They weren't filed in his name, and she would never have been able to locate them if she had decided to look. Obviously, he planned to come back some day and work them.

Jordan scanned the clearing grown dark under the approaching storm. ''So, where's Bailey?''

Gabrielle would rather cut out her tongue than tell him.

Sarah apparently took Gabrielle's silence for consent to inform Jordan. ''Papa left us the day after Aunt Gabrielle came. He said he wasn't ever comin' back.'' She stopped and looked up at Gabrielle as if seeking permission to continue.

''Go on,'' Jordan prompted.

''There's a real mean man that's comin' today. He says my papa owes him money, and we have to pay him. We don't have enough. But the Lord promised He'd take care of it, so we're not worryin'.''

Jordan, looking puzzled, turned to Gabrielle. ''You mean Bailey borrowed money from that bear-mauler, Pasket, and left you to pay?''

"I don't know his name, but Mr. Bailey did leave, owing a great deal of money to a rather disreputable person," she said.

"Well, finding that no-account Bailey won't be hard and, with his natural-born greed, I can clear those claims. As for Pasket, he'll be no trouble once he's paid." Jordan patted the battered case, then replaced it on his saddle.

Then in a sudden change of mood, his voice dropped to a disturbingly low pitch. "It's over, Gabby." Her heart plummeted. What was he saying? "It's over—the gambling, the boozing, the fast-living women—they were substitutes, anyway, to fill too many empty hours. You need to know that. But I've found something . . . Someone . . ."

He fixed his gaze on her as though memorizing each feature and as he did so, the harsh planes of his face softened. The wistful longing she had seen briefly shadow his features at various times now set itself firmly in place.

Jordan dropped to one knee. "Sarah, would you come to me?" he asked gently. She walked eagerly to him, and he sat her on his other knee, bent to receive her. He ran a gentle tracing finger around her face as though to sketch its shape.

"You are most definitely a miniature of your Aunt Gabby. Your face is the same shape, and you have the same enchanting musical voice."

"I do?"

He nodded and looked over the head of the child and deep into Gabrielle's eyes. "Those wide brown eyes are the softest, most gentle brown, and they light with shining sparks of amber when you're happy."

Sarah wrapped her little arms around Jordan's shoulders, and Gabrielle felt the longing, the need to do the same.

Jordan's eyes never wavered from Gabrielle's face. "Your skin's so soft, and your hair catches golden glints in candlelight."

Gabrielle's hand strayed to the chignon, neat and firm at the base of her neck. —

"When you smile, it's like turning on the sun. You're the most beautiful person I've ever known." Jordan folded Sarah to him and kissed her tenderly on the forehead. "I need your strength and wisdom to help heal me and make me whole." His gaze intensified as though with his eyes he felt he could burn his message on Gabrielle's heart. "I love you with all my being as I have never loved another."

Sarah looked up into his face and breathed, "I love you, too." Then lowering her eyes, she tucked her head into the curve of his neck.

The throbbing, soundless interval filled with a rush of wind through the trees which billowed Gabrielle's skirt, transported her to the top of a gossamer spiral staircase where Jordan waited. There, in their magic space, she surrendered to the promises his eyes held.

A meadow lark's unexpected trill caused her breath to catch, made her heart leap, made the world real again. Made her want to touch him. Made her reach a hand out to him.

He rose, still holding Sarah in his arms, and walked to stand beside Gabrielle and Amy. He slipped his hand around hers. She felt the calloused palm, hard and warm, close over hers . . . vital, strong, protecting.

Gabrielle let the joy at his touch flood through her, fill her senses, warm her heart.

Then parting the bond their hands had fashioned, she lifted Amy into her arms. Jordan encircled Gabrielle's shoulder with his arm and held her tightly to him.

Sarah reached, took Amy's hand and united the four of them. "God took care of us just fine, Amy," she said, a wide delighted smile wreathing her face.

Jordan looked at Gabrielle. "Yes, Sarah. God is here to guide our lives and answer all our prayers.

And He sent me to help Him. You don't ever have to be lonely or afraid again."

Gabrielle raised her eyes to his, felt the deep, secure, abiding love between them, sensed their shared faith, touched her cheek against the rough homespun sleeve, remembered the taste of his kiss, heard the low rumble of thunder in the distance.

"A storm is brewing. It's getting chilly," she said. "We'd best go inside to wait for the sun."

MEET THE AUTHOR

MARYN LANGER is a delightful lady, crammed with creativity! So full of fancy and tall tales is she that one would never suspect she spends her days teaching math to classrooms of kids, nor that she has written textbooks in her chosen field. She confesses, however, that her mind, whether asleep or awake, cannot help creating wonderful characters from the past, whose lives reflect her own strong Christian faith and fortitude.

Mrs. Langer resides with her husband in Albion, Idaho. WAIT FOR THE SUN is her first work of romantic fiction—but not her last! Look for MOON FOR A CANDLE, to be published in October.

A Letter To Our Readers

Dear Reader:

Pioneering is an exhilarating experience, filled with opportunities for exploring new frontiers. The Zondervan Corporation is proud to be the first major publisher to launch a series of inspirational romances designed to inspire and uplift as well as to provide wholesome entertainment. In order that we might better contribute to your reading enjoyment, we would appreciate your taking a few minutes to respond to the following questions and return to:

> Anne Severance, Editor
> Serenade/Saga Books
> 749 Templeton Drive
> Nashville, Tennessee   37205

1. Did you enjoy reading WAIT FOR THE SUN?
   - ☐ Very much. I would like to see more books by this author!
   - ☐ Moderately
   - ☐ I would have enjoyed it more if _____

2. Where did you purchase this book? _____

3. What influenced your decision to purchase this book?
   - ☐ Cover
   - ☐ Title
   - ☐ Publicity
   - ☐ Back cover copy
   - ☐ Friends
   - ☐ Other _____

4. Please rate the following elements from 1 (poor) to 10 (superior):

☐ Heroine   ☐ Plot
☐ Hero   ☐ Inspirational theme
☐ Setting   ☐ Secondary characters

5. Which settings would you like to see in future Serenade/Saga Books?

_____   _____

_____   _____

6. What are some inspirational themes you would like to see treated in future books?

_____   _____

_____   _____

7. Would you be interested in reading other Serenade/Serenata or Serenade/Saga Books?

☐ Very interested
☐ Moderately interested
☐ Not interested

8. Please indicate your age range:

☐ Under 18   ☐ 25–34   ☐ 46–55
☐ 18–24   ☐ 35–45   ☐ Over 55

9. Would you be interested in a Serenade book club? If so, please give us your name and address:

Name _____

Occupation _____

Address _____

City _____ State _____ Zip _____

Serenade Saga Books are inspirational romances in historical settings, designed to bring you a joyful, heart-lifting reading experience.

Serenade Saga books available in your local bookstore:

Watch for other books in the *Serenade Saga* series coming soon:

Serenade Serenata Books are inspirational romances in contemporary settings, designed to bring you a joyful, heart-lifting reading experience.

Serenade Serenata books available in your local bookstore:

Watch for other books in both the *Serenade Serenata* (contemporary) series coming soon: